THE HIDDEN BLADE

J. MANOA

EPIC
Escape

An Imprint of EPIC Press
EPICPRESS.COM

The Hidden Blade
Werewolf Council: Book #2

Written by J. Manoa

Copyright © 2018 by Abdo Consulting Group, Inc.

Published by EPIC Press™
PO Box 398166
Minneapolis, MN 55439

All rights reserved.

Printed in the United States of America.

International copyrights reserved in all countries.
No part of this book may be reproduced in any form without
written permission from the publisher. EPIC Press™ is trademark
and logo of Abdo Consulting Group, Inc.

Cover design by Candice Keimig & Neil Klinepier
Images for cover art obtained from iStockPhoto.com
Edited by Ryan Hume

LIBRARY OF CONGRESS CATALOGING-IN-PUBLICATION DATA
Names: Manoa, J., author.
Title: The hidden blade / by J. Manoa.
Description: Minneapolis, MN : EPIC Press, 2018. | Series: Werewolf council ; #2
Summary: A grisly murder rocks the town of Stumpvale. Nate learns that he is a part of a
  historic pact between werewolves and those who watch over them. Meanwhile, Riley finds a
  unique way to recover from the accident that nearly killed her.
Identifiers: LCCN 2016946214 | ISBN 9781680764994 (lib. bdg.)
  | ISBN 9781680765557 (ebook)
Subjects: LCSH: Friendship—Fiction. | Murder—Fiction. | Werewolves—Fiction. | Young
  adult fiction.
Classification: DDC [Fic]—dc23
LC record available at http://lccn.loc.gov/2016946214

EPICPRESS.COM

For Lara

PROLOGUE

THE METAL RAIL WAS COOL ON THE BACK OF HIS neck, but the hard edge dug into his skin. His feet were crossed at the ankles on the other rail of the train track. He stared up at the sky. Just enough light remained that the stars barely peeked through a tinge of blue. The wind through the leaves was a steady but slight applause in every direction. The scent of the forest surrounded him.

"I wouldn't do that if I were you," she said.

"I'll feel the train coming from miles away," he replied.

"No, I mean I wouldn't touch the rail with my

bare skin like that." She motioned toward where his neck made contact with the metal. "This thing is like a hundred years old."

"So?"

"That's a hundred years of dirt and grease and like, animal . . . stuff." She cringed and twitched with disgust. "Sick."

"Not that bad," he said, feeling the metal press uncomfortably. "It's actually kinda nice," he bluffed.

"Whatever."

He pushed himself up quickly. He ran one finger over the track where his head had been. In the lingering light he could see where his fingerprint darkened with dirt. "It's fine," he said.

She turned to walk atop the rail, putting her arms out like a child trying to balance. He cleaned his dirty finger on the leg of his jeans. He licked his other hand and wiped at the back of his neck, partly to remove any dirt, partly to rub away the stinging indent left in the skin.

"Getting kinda dark," she said, one leg rotating

in front of the other, arms still stretched for balance. He watched as folds in her skirt shifted with the movement. The light caught the soft texture of her leggings.

"We should probably get going."

"Why?" he said. His long steps landed on every other wooden beam in the ground.

She stopped and turned to him. She wobbled but recovered her balance. "Because it's getting dark," she said. "Weren't you listening?"

He kicked a few rocks off the next beam. "Dark is good," he said.

Her face was mostly in shadow, but she gave the same exaggerated shrug and head-lift that she always did when she rolled her eyes at him. "Maybe in the car, Liam, but not out here."

"In that case we should go back right now," he said, quickening his pace.

She giggled slightly while allowing herself to slide off the rail.

"What time do your parents want you home tonight?" he asked as he stepped closer.

She shrugged. "Anytime," she replied. The emerging starlight struck the corner of her eye, giving it a mischievous glint.

"So I can keep you until Dawn comes?" He'd made a similar joke before, while wiping away the fog which had gathered on his windshield after they'd spent an hour in the car in the elementary school parking lot.

"In that case I'd never get home," she replied.

"Ouch," he said, moving one hand to wrap around her hip. She slid away.

He paused a moment to huff. "Why?" he said as the wind kicked up around them.

She stopped a few feet away and turned toward him again, crossing her arms. She was almost entirely in shadow to him now, framed by the streetlight of the intersection far behind her. The car was at least four minutes away by foot: turn left where the tracks crossed the road to Juneau, and walk a couple hundred more feet to the recreation-area parking for hiking trails on this side of the nature preserve. Parking wouldn't close until midnight, so at least another half hour, possibly later since it was just now getting dark. If he was lucky then, the little patch of dirt along the side of the road back into town wouldn't be occupied, this week. It was private enough in the car. Might be too soon to return to the elementary school lot, so maybe one of the other dirt roads. There was never much traffic outside the town at night. Or inside really.

As he moved closer to her, he could see her hands rubbing her crossed arms. He reached out again, striding forward faster. She shifted away once more. He exhaled his frustration. She giggled.

The wind lowered into a steady murmur. He heard the quick crunch of the gravel under his steps. The streetlights drew closer. Her arms remained tight, but her skirt swayed with every motion of her thin hips. In the light her legs looked long and straight, like the track rails. He felt his foot slide off the edge of a small rock. He looked down to watch his feet, his light gray sneakers visible in the dark.

He heard a rolling rumble nearby. He turned to listen over his shoulder. It was there. A low, rolling sound. He glanced back for a headlight but saw nothing other than the tracks disappearing into the dark and the slight motion of trees blowing in the wind. It didn't sound like the train anyway: too low and quiet, not enough vibration. The sound was more like an engine, like a motorcycle idling a couple of streets over. It was far enough away that he couldn't see it, but close enough to know it was there. It drew closer. Not rumbling. Breathing. Liam quickened his steps, stomping on the wooden beams loud enough that Dawn glanced back at him.

"What—" she said. A long tremble cut her off. A growl. Unmistakable. He looked back to find darkness and nothing else. His steps quickened once more. He glanced between the tracks ahead and those behind. He put one hand on her back to propel her forward.

"Stop pushing me," she said, her footsteps clumsy on the gravel. He clasped onto her shoulder, still pressing ahead. "Stop!" she said again, squirming away.

"Come on," he said as he moved past her.

"Pushing me isn't gonna get you laid any sooner," she said, stopping on one of the beams. "You need to like—"

Something faded in from the darkness behind her. A mass slightly lighter than the black of the night grew larger as it approached. A pair of red eyes struck him.

"Run!" Liam yelled as he took off.

The gravel crunched under his steps. His feet trembled uneasily as the rocks shifted beneath him. He heard the thud of a wooden beam. He kept his head down as he ran, trying to plan his steps while keeping speed. He glanced back. Dawn was barely visible in the darkness. "Liam!" she yelled. "Liam!" He kept running. His feet were blurs in his vision.

He heard a roar that shook through his bones. Then a scream that pierced his ears like an ice pick.

He couldn't help looking back.

She was gone. The shadowed mass spanned almost the entire track. It seemed smaller, low but long. Liam heard a sound of tearing fabric. "No," he muttered to himself. He heard a sound of ripping flesh. "Please, God, no." He heard a sound of thick liquid hitting metal. "No, no." The mass moved with every rip and splatter. A rolling growl slowly rose. The figure twisted as a blur.

The red eyes glowed in his direction.

He ran once more. He looked out where the streetlights cast dull yellow on the dirt and green on the road ahead. He felt his foot slip off the rocks. He kept running, limping as the pain entered his ankle.

He heard the rolling growl in the back of his head. The tearing, ripping, splattering sounds lingered behind him. He didn't look back.

He stayed focused on the intersection ahead, the green traffic lights and the raised gates where the tracks met the road, red reflectors lining the top of the arm. They vanished as he turned the corner from the track.

He felt the red glow chase him down the road.

CHAPTER 1

"MAYBE IF I GET REALLY GOOD WITH THESE, then I'll be able to do handstands and cartwheels with them," Riley said, patting the crutches leaning next to her against the bench.

Nate didn't answer. He looked across the street at the Chase Bank on the corner where a trash can was chained to the lightpost. This was the spot where he had previously seen the man they called "Highlander," who he knew now as Father Vigilius. Nate kept his hands folded in his lap, his right thumb slowly rubbing his left palm.

"Probably just need more practice with them,"

Riley continued, glancing to where Nate rubbed the back of his hand as he stared across the street. "I'll probably get good with these things right when I don't need them anymore. Just like that time."

Nate's eyes fixed on the corner across from them. A cold wind blew past, lifting a discarded napkin from the asphalt and onto the curb. The napkin pressed flat against the base of the streetlight. It fell as the wind died down. Nate continued staring.

He'd barely faced her all morning. Of course, they were sitting on a bench facing the same direction, not at a table where they were meant to face each other. Did they normally sit in a way that let them face each other? Not looking at her might've been a clue that he was withholding something. So would looking at her too much.

"If you're planning to rob the place then you should be less conspicuous," Riley offered.

Still silent. Still not looking.

"Get blueprints or something," she muttered, glancing from him to the ground a few feet in front of them, where the brick path of her building ended and the grass led to the curb alongside the road. "Like they did in *Heat*."

"Sorry," Nate said.

He peeked at Riley for a second before shifting back to the ground.

"For what?" she said.

He blinked a couple of times quickly. "I mean, sorry? I wasn't listening."

"I was just playing," she said, still looking at the grass ahead. "That you were plotting something . . . unseemly."

"Unseemly?" he asked, following her gaze to the grass.

"Yeah, like robbing the bank or . . ." She shifted to take some weight off of her leg. They sat on opposite sides of the bench staring in the same direction. "Never mind," she said.

"All right," he said.

Silence came between them. The distance from the two ends of the bench seemed infinitely wider than it was two months before. Riley looked up from the grass to the hairdresser's salon across the street. She'd never gotten around to redoing the blond streak, which had all but completely faded from her hair. Her hand came up to trace that strand behind her ear. She lifted her hand once more to feel the dents and cracks at the side of her face. Several small marks filled the spaces between the three carved scars. The highest of the three arched down and across her temple and into the hairline. The middle one began back from her eyebrow and led to where a piece had been ripped from the inside of her ear at the tragus (a word she didn't know before getting stitched). The lowest, shortest scar ran one inch from the top of her cheekbone. She couldn't stop touching them. She couldn't stop staring at them. She couldn't stop feeling like other people couldn't stop staring at them.

The blare of police sirens started from somewhere behind Riley's building. It grew louder, bouncing off the road next to them.

"What the hell?" Nate said, leaning to see around the tree at the corner.

"Uh oh," Riley, "they're onto you."

Nate twisted around quickly. His mouth hung slightly open as though stupefied.

The sirens grew louder until they were almost all either Riley or Nate could hear.

"Your plot to rob the bank," Riley yelled over the echoing noise.

He seemed frozen for a moment before turning to watch as the pair of police cars rushed down the road and into the distance.

"Right," Nate said, leaning to the side as he tracked the cars down the road.

"Probably a break-in or something," Riley offered. "A dumb prank by bored kids."

Nate slouched back into the bench as the sirens faded. He resumed staring at nothing.

Riley looked down at her hand, turning it to see the spots left in her forearm and under her bicep. Defensive wounds, Dr. Rubin had called them. He had blocked his face with his palm to demonstrate. He said by the time she reached her mid-twenties the little craters would be tiny gaps in the skin while the scars would be thin lines, and by the time she was his age they'd blend in with the wrinkles. None of that made them any smaller or less noticeable now. It didn't make her stop tracing them as though they'd have suddenly disappeared, taking all that'd happened with them. It didn't stop others from staring at them before glancing away like she wouldn't notice.

"Oh," Nate said, jolting from his position, "I ended up rewatching *Easy Rider* the other day."

She raised her eyes to him. She shifted her weight again to sit up straight.

"Much better the second time," he said. "I think knowing what happens with the characters and how sudden it is adds a sort of . . ." He thought for a moment, head tilted up toward the electric wires running over the sidewalk. "I want to say joy . . . and sorrow . . . to everything that comes before." His pupils drifted upward. "But then I guess that's the same for every movie once you know what happens." His gaze turned to her. Her eyes, not her scars. "I guess I just felt for the characters more this time, knowing they'd be treated so viciously in the end. Made me angry." Then he looked away, almost sheepishly, as though it just occurred to him that maybe it wasn't the best idea to mention a movie where the main characters die in a road incident to a girl still recovering from her own fatal crash.

"That's always how it is with movies where the main character dies in the end," she said, nodding at him. "Feels like . . . you should have seen it coming."

"No one deserves to be treated like that," he said, wandering in his own world again, "hunted for nothing."

"Not them but there could be others who . . . " She stopped talking as an itch rose just above her left knee, and she pressed down on the gray padding between the Velcro straps connecting the hard plastic encasing her upper leg. There was a gap over the knee for a pair of hinged rods that attached to a plastic boot with the same gray padding and Velcro straps as the upper cast.

Dr. Rubin said the entire contraption was meant to help her readjust to walking, once the leg was strong enough to support her weight again. It also allowed her to remove the cast when she showered or slept, as long as she was careful and kept the leg elevated. All she cared about was that it wasn't the cumbersome lump of plaster she'd been lugging for weeks. The thing was so solid and heavy. With a good enough swing on the crutches, she could probably cave in one of the lockers at school. Plus, she could finally scratch her leg when it itched and the cast was off, as long as she was careful.

"This is much better," she said. Her mind flashed to the other contraption she'd been given following her accident. Both had straps, one Velcro and the other leather. Both were created to fit one of her limbs: this one, plastic around the back and side of her leg; the other a flat metal plate over her forearm with a rounded piece over the back of her hand to guard against another accident, and thin wire to a pressure release over her palm. Only, one of them concealed an eight-inch blade.

"What?" Nate said as though snapping back to reality.

"This," she said, tapping the soft side of the cast.

Half of her leg was straps and pads, the other half, hard plastic. The padding almost matched the pants she wore that day, one of five pairs of sweats her mother bought and cut one leg off of so Riley could wear them with the cast. Hell, she could even wear them to gymnastics practice, if she felt like having one leg completely covered and one completely exposed. If she ever did gymnastics again. Dr. Rubin had told her not to worry about gymnastics for now, only worry about healing.

"You wouldn't believe the amount of hair that grew in two months."

Nate chuckled. "You have no idea," he said.

"Well, probably not as much as there is for a guy, but it was not nice."

He shrugged. "Cosmetic," he said, glancing once more this time to the scars at the side of her face before quickly looking away. She assumed the glance was unconscious. "As long as it works properly."

She sighed. "We'll see about that."

"Yeah," he sighed as well. "I mean, it should, right?"

Silence took over. Riley ran through a list of topics in her head. They'd talked about movies enough already, had to be something better. What did they normally talk about back when they were just two high school kids? Probably no important news about their classmates. The ones who could afford it were off somewhere on vacation; those who couldn't were delivering pizza, or behind a cash register; and everyone else was probably wasting time some other way. None of them would do anything worth talking about. Didn't stop them before.

Sitting in front of her place like this, which one of them would prompt the conversation? Trying to push him to talk might make it seem that there was something she really wanted to tell him. Or being quiet might. It shouldn't be so hard to remember what normal was.

Nate inhaled sharply. "I'm sorry," he said.

Riley closed her eyes. She took a deep breath. It was exactly what she didn't want to hear.

"I am."

"You keep saying that," she said.

"Yeah," he said, no longer even trying to make eye contact with her, "because I am."

"There are some things you can't control, okay?" she said. "You weren't even there."

His gaze remained averted from her, more obvious now than ever before. Maybe this is what he'd been holding in.

"I know you think you can protect me all the time but you can't. There are some things that just . . . " She saw his eyes close. A pained look came upon his face, as though she'd told him they couldn't be friends anymore. "That are beyond what we can do. It's like . . . fate or something."

She took another deep breath. He shook his head as though in regret.

"It's all anyone wants to talk about these days," she said, turning away from him. "My mom won't stop asking about how I feel. My doctor keeps trying to get me to go to a counselor. Every message I get from everyone is asking if I'm okay and if there's something I need. Everyone except you"—she glanced at the bench between them—"and I like that. You're like the only person who isn't . . . obsessed with trying to make me . . . better, or something."

Her mind flashed to her hair hanging from her head, a mess of dark strands and one blond streak on the SUV's ceiling. In the next seat Remy's face was more blood than skin. His parents had come to visit her in the hospital. They'd said he was dead on impact, before the fire started. At least he wasn't burned alive. At least it was quick.

"It happened," she said, her mind returning to the bench. "This is . . . the path we're on now."

Nate blinked at her for a moment, then away.

"No way to change that."

He sighed as he settled back into his own world. Probably best to leave him lost this time.

Another siren sounded from farther away. Neither of them turned toward it.

"I should go," she said as the silence returned. "I need to gather my things for PT."

"How's that going?" Nate asked without facing her.

"It's mostly pool work for now, kicking against a wall." He nodded but may not have been listening, again. "Another good thing about this." She tapped her cast. He didn't see.

"All right," he said, standing up. "I'll let you get to it."

Riley pushed one arm firmly against the bench

while the other pulled from the top of the crutches. She leaned her weight onto the better leg. She closed her eyes, wincing as pain still surged through. Just standing caused her to breathe heavily. Her eyes opened. She saw Nate quickly drop the hand he'd extended for her. His eyes lowered as well.

She balanced on one foot and a pair of crutches. She rolled her head side to side until he looked at her. She attempted a smile. "Come on," she said, "proper goodbye."

He straightened up and put his arms out. She hopped forward slightly, both crutches propped under one arm. They hugged. She squeezed her arms around him. It felt like his back had gotten firmer in the couple of weeks since they'd last been able to hang out. They separated.

"Let me know how it goes," he said as he stepped away.

"Sure," she said. She placed the crutches and pivoted in the direction of her building. She crutched to the base of the stairs and then hopped onto each of the three steps and then to the entrance keypad.

She didn't have to look back. She knew he was still there, waiting, watching until she entered the building. Even now, after everything that had happened, he was still looking out for her. Maybe one day she'd be able to look out for him.

CHAPTER 2

H E HATED LYING TO HIS MOM, BUT THE PHONE call sounded urgent.

"The Council would like to see you," said the woman in a tone so flat it could have been a computer program, "three o'clock." He turned the truck around and headed back to town. Nate didn't notice the street signs as he turned off Haida and onto Cedar. Most people didn't even use the names of the streets. Take the second right after the museum, head over Big Bridge toward the high school and take a left after Three Bears, things like that.

He remembered running through the town with

Riley over his shoulder, almost two months before. He hadn't even seen—actually seen—the places as he passed, he'd simply known where he needed to go. He did the same thing now, driving his mother's truck, only there were no burning scents for him to follow, there was simply memory, familiarity, and habit. As much as things had changed since that night, the town itself and most of the people in it had remained exactly the same. With a few exceptions.

He pulled into the parking lot sandwiched between the plaza and the museum. He stretched to look down the winding cobblestone pathway that led to the fountain in the center of the plaza. Other paths branched off to the north, south, and west, parallel in their turns for a symmetrical design. Between the four paths were spaces filled with trees, bushes, flowers, benches, and a couple pavilions. A low, wide bush lined the inner side of the tall iron fence that surrounded the entire plaza, and the gates at each of the entrances were closed between sundown and sunrise. Summer gatherings could go on until almost midnight. Winter gatherings didn't happen. His mother had once told him that the layout of the park, with its symmetrical paths and unorganized vegetation, was meant to suggest both balance and chaos. The things we can control and the things we can't.

He took a moment to gather himself as he stood at the base of the long staircase to the museum entrance. He'd already told them everything he knew about that night. Some of them, like Councilor Maier, he'd told more than once. Yet they still called him in. He checked that the truck's door was locked before beginning the walk to the museum.

The stairs, three sets of three steps with long landings separating each set, bisected a pair of six-foot-tall walls covered in bas-reliefs of wildlife from the area. The carvings were framed as rough equals of each other, different species within the same family: a caribou and an elk at the farthest edges of the wall, a coyote and a fox, a lynx and a mountain lion, an eagle and a hawk, a moose and a bison, a weasel and a shrew, a seal on the shore and a breeching whale, a squirrel and a rabbit, two bears with different patterns carved into their hides, and in the middle, framing the staircase, were a pair of humans—or what had always looked to him like humans—facing each other with a gap between. The one on the left wore a jacket, carried a satchel, and had long hair, while the one on the right wore shorter sleeves and carried a rifle. They both had the same features carved into their faces and they both held one hand out to the other at the very edge of the wall. When he was very young, Nate joked that it looked like they were about to high-five. He couldn't see it as anything else until he was first summoned by the Council to comment on the events leading up to and following the incident.

The gray stone of the museum came into view as he ascended the stairs. A short colonnade led to the three double-door entrances. A large, triangular roof topped the columns, its peak aligned with the main building. Windows marked the three levels of the museum as more columns lined its front, like a fence isolating the building from its surroundings, as though it weren't already divided by its imposing, monochromatic structure against the weathered signs and open entrances of what passed for downtown in Stumpvale.

Nate kept his head down as he passed a few visitors on their way out. He held the door open for a young boy and his father to pass through before heading in. The front room was a shallow rectangle with a reception desk in front of a large wall lined with pictures and signs pointing toward bathrooms. A set of double doors on each side of the reception desk led into the museum itself. Nate waited as the pair of women in front of him moved from the desk to the gallery entrance.

"Good afternoon, Nathaniel," said the little woman seated behind the ticket booth. She had short and very white hair, huge glasses, deeply cracked lips, and smelled strongly of coffee. Strongly enough that he could smell it even now.

Nate reached into his pocket for his membership card.

"Go right ahead, dear," said Vera. Or maybe it was Dorothy. One of those old lady names.

"Thank you," he said, already stepping toward the entrance, past a list of major donors and contributors. The third name from the bottom was Patrick Wallace. Two names above it was Clarence McKnight.

Nate was greeted by the blue whale skeleton hanging over the center of the gallery. Beneath it ran the central hall of the main gallery with a wide, octagonal display of information about "Leonard" directly below the whale's skull. His father's name was on that display as well. Other exhibits branched off from the hall into small rooms of glass cases filled with dug up bones of both animals and humans, mostly found during oil exploration. Nate craned his neck back as he walked. He stared at the huge bones of the whale's jaw, the way it jutted out from a pair of hinges, the curve of the rib cage and spine, the relatively tiny bones at the extremes of the fins, the nooks which fit the vertebrae together, and the smoother textures of plastic pieces which filled in for lost bones. It was almost hard to believe that something so big, so different from himself, could actually exist in the world. He continued through another pair of double doors leading to Gallery B.

The second gallery was less dramatic and had several smaller exhibit areas branching from the narrow central hall. Lining the path through the gallery were detailed photographs of mountains and trees, rivers and valleys, oceans and glaciers. Outer exhibits focused on specific themes: endangered species of plants and animals, rare native fish, and two models showing how the polar ice cap has receded in the last fifty years. Nate always found these exhibits more depressing than informative.

It wasn't until last month, his second time summoned to the Council, that he realized depression was the point. Everything within this building—the dead animals posed behind glass, the butterflies framed on the walls, the whale bones hanging from the ceiling, the photos of where the forest ended from years of logging and oil leaking into natural streams—was intended as a rebuke. It was meant to remind visitors, locals and tourists, human or otherwise, just how destructive people could be. It was an ornate "you suck" to humankind.

Gallery B ended with a long, empty space, like that at the very front of the museum. A fire exit and freight entrance occupied the gap behind the last exhibition. One narrow door along the rear wall led to what Nate had always assumed was storage. Security guards sat at both of these rear exits. Nate withdrew the membership card from his pocket, checking behind him as he approached the chubby guard leaning against the rear wall. He pressed the back of the card up to the door lock, and the red light flashed green. The guard nodded as Nate opened the door. "Mr. Wallace," he said.

Voices grew louder as he progressed through the hallway behind the door. He tapped a couple of the metal handles sticking out of wooden file cabinets that lined both sides of the passage. Little cards with years printed on them were slid into metal frames along their faces. Inside the drawers were birth records, death certificates, proofs of sale, and other such documents dating as far back as the founding of the town in 1883, more than one hundred years after the establishment of the Nobilitate Nobis Accord.

"—can't be tolerated," a voice boomed from within the chamber ahead. "They are attempting to scapegoat us."

During his first trip into this room, accompanied by his mother, he was shown documents from England, France, Germany, some from Norway and Sweden, and even a few from Russia. They'd been carried around for generations until those families eventually settled in the town, attracted by its isolation and security. The world could be a frightening place for people like them.

"This is a clear violation of our agreement," the voice continued, "and it must be dealt with immediately."

He had even seen his own certificate of live birth during that first visit, prior to having to speak about the night of the accident. The paper was smaller and grittier than he expected. A red stamp at the bottom had an uneven image of a round sun with triangular rays extending from it. The words "Nobilitate Nobis—By the blood we are bound" formed a rim around the image.

"That is precisely the worst thing we can do," said another voice which Nate recognized as that of High Councilor Ulrich, a retired defense attorney who had served on the City Council for several years. His voice remained calm and measured as he spoke. "We're better using our connections and authority to determine the cause of this tragedy before acting."

An open doorway led to a smaller room with more cabinets along each wall and a display case in the center. Under the locked glass and in a series of carved insets were the pages of the original town charter which established Stumpvale as a place of "brotherhood" and "kinship" and a "sanctuary for those whom the world has forgotten." Basically, Nate had thought as he looked over the fancy cursive writing, it was a place where his kind— werewolves, Fenrei, however they preferred to be called—could get away from people. At least, that's what it was in the beginning.

"The action has already been taken," the other man, Councilor Maier, said in his typically commanding tone. "The blackrobes have taken the initiative. We must react."

Nate leaned to see around the corner into the main chamber at the end of the hall. A circle of around twenty people stood in the middle of the domed chamber. Nate immediately recognized the faces of his former history teachers, Mr. Clarkson and Mrs. Wald, among those lined up in front of the rear wall. From behind, Nate could see Ulrich's large bald spot rimmed by dark gray hair, a few small sunspots left in the skin of his scalp. He stood a half step in front of the tall, dark woman next to him. Across the circle, a half step from his own place, was Matthew Maier, tall and surprisingly broad for a man in his sixties or seventies. He had a wide nose and chin that looked as though any fist which landed on it would break. A wolf hovered just over Maier's right shoulder.

"Reaction alone is not a virtue, Councilor," Ulrich replied.

Nate almost stepped back at the sight. The deep red eyes set beneath a heavy brow, the jaw extending from a powerful hinge in the back of the face, the curved spine into a long neck with a head big enough to swallow his forearm whole. It was still jarring to see one of his own kind. This particular wolf had thick fur protruding from under its chin and rough points over the top of its head and along its shoulders. The beast—it would probably take years to break that idea—seemed to growl through every breath, and leaned forward slightly in a way that made it only a few inches taller than anyone else.

"We must have the proper reaction," Ulrich continued.

Over the heads of the crowd Nate could see the tapestry which occupied the entire wall at the rear of the chamber. Village homes burned in bright red and orange fabrics. Slightly stained whites showed crusaders marching along a dirt road, thrusting long spears and swords into the gray and brown beasts, and leaving bleeding bodies in their wake. In the foreground, which Nate could barely see between the people in the room, soldiers caped in white and gold stood in radiant glory as, hidden at the bottom of the tapestry, their enemies lay dismembered and bleeding. Nate remembered seeing the lower left corner during his first meeting with the Council, when the room was emptier than now. In the corner, almost a forgotten footnote, a tiny child stared through clawed fingers at a headless body curled in front of her.

"We first need to know whether it was the Order that perpetuated this crime. Then we must consider why. What would they ga—"

"And let's not forget his part in this." Maier stuck one stout finger in Nate's direction. He froze as every eye turned toward him. "His ignorance could have exposed us all."

"Yet it was our measured effort that assured the incident went unreported," Ulrich said, pulling some of the attention back from Nate. "Besides," he added, turning toward the opening behind him, "who among us had a flawless first change?"

"I was taught the ways of the Fenrei beforehand. I participated in the Feral Right before my first change." Maier replied as Ulrich motioned for Nate to join the group. He stepped aside to give him a place in the circle. Others shuffled over as he approached. "I didn't attempt to deny what I am."

"So you would deny that choice to others."

Maier locked his gaze toward Nate. The beard lining his chin had the same texture as hair carved into statues. His wrinkles were fine slivers with an old scar disappearing under his right eyebrow. "Those foolish enough to deny their gifts shouldn't endanger those who embrace them."

Nate felt his lip twitch. The wolf's red eyes glowed at him, like brake lights. The same red he saw in the floating face the night of the incident. Sister Dove.

"Yet, here he is," Ulrich said, turning toward Nate next to him. His lids drooped near the edges of his soft eyes. His beard was an inch of unkempt hair brightening from dark to light gray. "Exactly as summoned. Eager to participate and learn. He isn't denying his place. He's preparing for it."

Maier scoffed at this. "Only after his foolishness proved fatal."

Nate's fingers tensed. The wolf continued to stare. Nate thought he could hear a low growl, a steady rumble like the ground settling beneath the floor.

"If not for his actions"—the gunshot shook through Nate's mind, followed by the sounds of metal shredding across the asphalt, glass shattering, a hollow giggle, and the smell of smoke—"perhaps this incident wouldn't have—"

A bullet is a bullet, Ulrich had told him, no matter what it's made of. They are all potentially deadly. Any other idea is a fantasy.

"They forced me!" Nate yelled.

Ulrich pressed one arm across Nate's chest. Nate took a deep breath. He imagined cool air entering his body, just as Ulrich had instructed him to whenever he felt anger starting to build inside him.

"Let's leave Nathaniel out of this," Ulrich offered.

"Why?" Maier said, looking at the others gathered in the chamber. "The blackrobes haven't." He pointed toward Nate once more. "His run through the town was the opening they wanted. They have given clear provocation. This girl was just the first."

"They would have killed her!" Nate shouted. Ulrich's arm crossed him once more.

"There was another event this morning, son," Ulrich whispered, leaning closer. Nate glanced over quickly, catching Ulrich's pale blue eyes. "Along the railroad tracks."

"What?" Nate asked. He remembered the police sirens outside of Riley's house.

Maier let out one stunted laugh, "No surprise that pup remains unaware of what is happening right around him." The wolf grunted. Maier looked amusedly at others in the group. "It's particularly sad that such a tragedy wouldn't have occurred if the blackrobes didn't have an easy scapegoat."

Nate felt heat rising in the back of his throat as he looked at Maier. The wolf lingered a few steps from the councilor's side.

"This pup's recklessness has threatened our secrecy, and this council's tepid response to such actions has given the Order permission to conduct themselves as they please."

"I didn't even know what I was doing," Nate growled back at Maier, the heat spreading to his shoulders. "I didn't want to know, and I wish I never had to."

"Again he denies his birthright." Maier waved one hand in dismissal. "The boy clearly learned from his mother."

"What the hell does that mean?" A glob of spit flew as Nate shouted across the gap in the crowd. He pressed forward against Ulrich's extended arm. The arm felt cold against the burn within his chest.

The large wolf pushed the others away to step into line with Maier.

"If your father were still alive perhaps none of this—"

"Enough!" Ulrich roared. He paused a moment for the echo of his voice to fade. "It is clear that this council is in no position to make a rational decision at this time. Councilor Maier's objection shall be noted. However, as speaker for this body, I do not feel that open hostilities against the Order are in our best interests at this time." Ulrich's view turned from Maier and all the way around to Nate before going back. "Instead, we will continue to use our connections within the city so that we may limit any chance of exposure to the general populace." Nate watched as the wolf across the room stepped back. Its ear twitched. "Are we in agreement?"

Several among the crowd nodded. "By the blood we are bound," they said one by one.

Maier was silent for a moment.

"Are we?" Ulrich repeated.

"By the blood we are bound," Maier said with a nod.

The gathering broke into smaller groups. Ulrich planted one hand on Nate's shoulder to pull him away from the others.

"You need to work on your control, son," Ulrich said after he and Nate were alone in a corner of the room. "The Council doesn't work if we aren't together. That's why I summoned you here, so that you could finally be a part of our community."

"Doesn't seem like he's interested in working together," Nate said, looking over at Maier, who stood with a couple of others. His wolf hovered over his shoulder.

"Councilor Maier is fulfilling an important role in our society. He may not seem it, but he is loyal. That's our way."

Nate had heard that before, during every previous visit to the back room of the museum.

"There was another incident this morning," Ulrich continued. "A young girl, about your age, was found dead on the train tracks. Descriptions of the body appear consistent with . . . our methods. I had hoped that maybe you knew something about this girl and her boyfriend that could aid our investigation into the matter."

Nate shook his head. "Didn't hear anything about it. I mean, other than a few sirens," he said. The entire department must have been going crazy over the first actual murder since before he was born. "I was with my friend Riley all morning."

"How is she? Recovering well?"

Nate nodded. "Seems to be."

"I imagine she'll be fine. I knew her father. He was," Ulrich paused as though in memory, "a man of tremendous conviction."

Nate pondered this a moment. He'd only ever heard of Mr. McKnight through Riley and others. Conviction was not a word which commonly came up.

"Dawn," Ulrich said, "Dawn Musgrave, that was her name. The girl who was found."

Nate furrowed his brow. "Dawn?"

"Did you know her?"

"I've seen her around," Nate replied, shaking his head, "but I never spoke to her or anything."

"How about the boyfriend? Liam Bailey."

Nate shook his head once again.

"So sad," he said. "How could something like that happen?"

"That's what we're trying to find out." Ulrich took a moment to glance around the room behind them before continuing. "I would like you to help with an investigation I've put together for tonight. You'll meet here at one before heading to the crime scene."

"I'm not sure I should. I . . . I'm not exactly," Nate searched for the right word, "skilled."

"We'll make sure the scene is clear long before you arrive. This is the perfect opportunity for you to apply some of things we've been practicing." Ulrich stepped back to slap Nate's shoulder. "You've done well so far, son," he said with an assuring smile. "But," he looked across the room Nate had shouted over during the meeting, "you have a lot left to learn." His smile disappeared. "A lot."

Nate puzzled at how Ulrich could even think of smiling while talking about investigating a murder. Although he'd never spoken to Dawn, barely seen her enough to even picture her in his mind, it was still . . . baffling. One day she was alive and the next gone. Just gone. It happens like that sometimes, he thought. But that didn't mean it made sense. And sense or cause or an explanation wouldn't make it any less sad.

CHAPTER 3

RILEY GRUNTED AS SHE SHOULDERED OPEN THE car door. It was always awkward to pull her crutches between the seats of her mom's Honda. The cabin was barely long and tall enough, and lifting her mostly empty backpack from the footwell to the sidewalk outside, then reaching into the backseat to grab the crutches, angling the pair of metal sticks between front seats and swinging them around all made for an annoying, ungraceful movement. Added to that frustration was the discomfort of having to then slide forward, bend down to the backpack on the sidewalk, hang it on her shoulders, feeling the emptiness of nothing but her swimsuit and towel in the entire bag, and push up with her arms until the crutches were in place, all so she could simply stand and walk. Or what passed for walking when she had large plastic coverings over one entire leg and a pair of metal poles. Each step meant swinging one foot forward and catching herself from falling.

"Riley," her mother called from inside the car.

Riley pivoted on her good foot while scraping the toe of her walking cast.

"Riley."

Riley noticed the dark gray appearing at the roots of her mother's longer than shoulder-length hair. Probably time to get it dyed and cut again. The bags under her eyes had reappeared as well. Riley couldn't help but feel somewhat responsible for her mother looking so much older now than she had only a few weeks before, but there was nothing she could do about it. No regrets could change what happened. No promises could change what would happen.

"Don't rush yourself," her mother said, leaning with one hand on the passenger seat, "you'll get there." Sunlight streaming in through the windshield glistened off the gold watch she always wore on her way to work. She'd later remove it when she put on her hygienist scrubs.

"I know," Riley muttered as she inched away from the car.

"It'll take time," her mother replied, adding a reassuring nod, "but you'll recover."

Riley tucked the crutch into her armpit and pushed the car door shut as hard as she could with just her forearm and wrist. It closed with a hollow sound behind her. The car rolled a few feet before stopping again when her mother reached all the way across to push open the door.

"It's okay!" Riley heard through the crack, "I got it!" Just before the door slammed shut. She couldn't even generate the force to close a car door.

Riley felt the crutches vibrate with every impact on the sidewalk in front of the frosted glass windows of Green and Rivera Physical Therapy Services. The letters of their logo formed a rainbow over a horizon bisecting a sun. Riley assumed the sign itself was a test. Was it sunrise or sunset? Are you a positive person or a negative person? Will your therapy succeed or fail? If it fails, whose fault is that? Maybe it's because you didn't really try.

The plastic ends of each metal stick muffled the smack of her steps, a hollow sound vibrated through the empty shaft, followed by an airy tap of one foot and the occasional clunk of her boot's toe. Heavy-soft. Heavy-soft. She leaned against the door to enter, being careful not to lean so far that gravity would pull her down.

The office was an open space of exercise machines, stationary bikes, and massage tables, with a stack of stability balls in wooden frames tucked in the corner. A muscular guy followed an old man as he waddled between a pair of low parallel bars.

"Good afternoon, Ms. McKnight," said Brenda, the receptionist. She had the face of a bulldog and the wardrobe of someone who really liked putting sweaters on her bulldog. "Diane should be with you in a moment." She gestured toward a trio of seats lining the frosted window next to the door, and Riley crutched over. She set her weight to her right foot as she placed the crutches against the chair, turned on her heel, and braced her arms against the chair before lowering herself into it.

The old man grunted as he neared the end of the bars. She remembered practicing on bars last year, swinging up and over, releasing, and spinning and catching herself on the way down, swinging over and over, letting go into a pair of somersaults and a solid landing. Remember to smile. Make it look easy. Now she needed parallel bars just to walk, gritting her teeth and grunting all the way through.

A lady with a blond ponytail and a blue collared shirt, all three buttons open, stepped out of the small office in the rear of the center. "Good job, Mr. Hauser," she said as she strode past the old man. "Hey Riley," Diane said with a smile. "Ready to go?"

As Riley silently readied herself to press up from the chair once more, Diane stepped back to give her room. Riley tried not to show any effort, but she kept her hands gripped on the chair's arms for as long as she could.

"All right," Diane said, far too cheerfully. "Brenda, we'll be back in a couple of hours." She pulled the door open.

"I know," Brenda grumbled.

"So if anyone calls, tell them I've gone for a swim with my buddy Riley."

"I'll definitely do exactly that," she muttered as the door closed.

"Charlatan," Diane spat, stepping into the parking lot. Riley remained at the top of the slope up the curb as Diane walked to her little sedan, buttoning her shirt as she did.

Riley pulled the passenger-side door open until the bottom nearly scraped the ground. She dropped her backpack into the footwell, turned away from the seat and lowered onto it, wincing when her

56

thigh made contact. She pushed herself in with her good leg, angled her crutches between the front seats, and slammed the door closed. All that work just to sit down.

They rode in silence.

They drove from the therapy center onto Spruce Street, the one with the two Starbucks locations about three blocks from each other. "No, the other Starbucks," was the joke among most people she knew, even those who spent the summer working at the other "other" Starbucks. They passed the intersection with Haida, the empty lots near the end of the road, and on until Spruce stopped at the corner of Yupik with a few broken-down houses at the edge of the forest. Dirt tracks cut between two of the old houses. A chain blocked their progress. A sign hanging from the chain on a pair of small, metal loops read "NO ENTRY," as though it were shouting. Diane left the car to unlock and lower the chain. She kept the driver's door open as the car rolled by, then secured the chain once more before they continued down the dirt road.

The tracks wound through the forest. A few fallen trees came into view, left over from the last heavy snow. Riley could hear a couple of pebbles hit the bottom of the car, but not many. They moved at a good speed, enough that Riley felt the pull as they took the turns in the road, and she winced at the vibrations through the broken bone in her leg, until reaching another pair of posts with another chain, this time separating the forest from a wide clearing. Diane left the chain down this time.

An old barn took up most of the clearing, its doors also chained and covered with signs screaming at visitors. The barn walls were the brown-green-red color of rust. The roof was lined with brittle, broken metal. Flakes mingled with dirt on the ground below. The car circled to the side of the building, toward a large shed of moldy brick with a red, wooden door. The door had no lock and no handle. A fence of spiky rust ran between the two structures.

The car backed up so that the passenger door faced that of the shed.

Diane looked at the clock on the dashboard. "Eighty-seven minutes," she said.

Riley repeated the process of exiting a car. She bumped the door closed with her hip. It hit with more force than her mother's did. The car moved away slowly. Riley had no idea where Diane went during her sessions, but knew that she would be back in eighty-seven minutes.

Dirt softened the hollow sound of the crutches, but the uneven terrain made swinging forward less certain. The dirt could loosen and slide as Riley's weight shifted. She'd collapse onto her side. Hopefully her uninjured one. Luckily, the dirt wasn't hard enough to cause any serious damage. Unless she hit a rock, which was always possible. There was a time when she thought she understood what was possible. That was her last day walking. She reminded herself to scrape the dirt off the bottom of her crutches and shoe before meeting her mother again in front of the clinic.

She balanced on one crutch as she banged on the wooden door. She waited a few seconds before banging on it again, hard enough that it made the bottom of her fist ache. She faintly heard the jingle of keys from within the shed.

"Where are you?" asked the voice behind the door.

"Beneath the shroud," Riley answered.

"Where do you wish to be?"

"Bathed in the light."

There was a heavy clank and thud of a huge lock. The door creaked as it opened away from her. Riley felt the concrete in the vibration of the crutch as she stepped into the shed.

The tall man watched as she entered. He was partly hidden behind the door, but she could still see his blank face, eyes looking down at her expectantly. He closed the door after she entered.

The crutches echoed. Tubular bulbs ran parallel

to each wall, the little light bouncing off the empty brick, casting the center of the room into near darkness. A small pile of clothes and a mat were on the floor a few feet from a staircase leading downward, under the back of the shed and the soft ground beyond the wall. Riley cautiously approached the staircase, rolling foot to crutches, foot to crutches. The staircase led down far enough that it disappeared under the shed floor. Stone steps and a long way down. It would be enough of a fall to kill.

She took a deep breath. She lifted both of her crutches out, like bird's wings, and took a short hop to the first step. She tapped the toe of her plastic boot and slid into position for the next hop.

"If this is the greatest of your trials," the tall man said, watching her, "then your life will have been wasted."

Her legs ached by the time she reached the bottom of the stairs. It was good practice, she told herself, at least one leg will be strong . . . and even bigger than it already was. The last hop was a welcome one. She brought the crutches back down and pushed forward.

The brick walls came to arches over her, like the cloister of an old church, or the entrance of an ancient tomb. She heard a grunt in the distance, muffled by the rough surfaces, the pointed insets for lanterns, and the contours of the ceiling. Heavy breathing became louder as she progressed, audible between the heavy-soft pattern of her crutch and footsteps. There was a clank of metal. The hallway narrowed ahead as wooden cases ran along one wall. The first contained swords. Three-foot-long blades reflected the dim light diffusing through the glass covering. The hilts had simple crossguards, with leather wrapped around the handles and round, gray pommels. Sheathes were next to them, plain black with basic plating at the locket and chape. Nothing intricate. Not for stock weapons. Two swords were missing from the case, the sheathes left behind.

The next case contained two racks of shorter swords at the bottom and daggers on the top, sheathed and hanging by the crossguard. Again, basic weapons, but more of them than there were swords.

The third, and the one with wooden crossbeams overlaying the glass, had two shelves of flintlock pistols, their curved handles pointing out to anyone who happened by. The shelves ended with racks of old rifles and muskets, their firing mechanisms so clean and polished that they looked new despite the antiquated design. At the end of the line, with a greater separation between wooden slats, were four guns with shorter, wider barrels that flared out at the end. Blunderbusses. Thunder guns.

On the opposite wall, facing the glass cases as though keeping an eye on their contents, was a series of portraits. The insets with their lanterns separated the pictures into sets of three. The first of the portraits depicted a severe man with a clean-shaven face, a long forehead, and small eyes. He wore a white shirt with a gold cross securing its high collar, and a black cloak draped over his shoulders, held in place by a pair of black threads which hung lightly over his collarbones. The paint was faded and cracked in places. The simple wooden frame had several dents as though it had bounced around over the years. The clearest part was the nameplate under the picture: Father Benedict the Second.

The next face was younger, almost gentle, dull blue eyes, fuzzy hair, and the rounded features of a large child. Father Innocent the Third, according to the nameplate. The third portrait, that of Father Leo the Seventh, was almost completely faded. Only the outline shadow of his face and the black of the cloak covering his shoulders remained. Six other portraits followed, all of them variations of the same theme: stern-looking men in high white collars and black cloaks, the black hood becoming more visible as the paintings became more recent. Father Sylvester the Fourth replaced the gold cross with a symbol which resembled a sun burst with a series of lines connecting the two ends of the pointed rays through the round center, as though the rays were lying on top of each other. Riley knew that the first portrait in the next set was Father Pius the Third. She hesitated a moment before glancing at it.

Her father stared back at her.

He looked different with his black hair brushed back, thick and shining like a helmet, or like a character from a Scorsese mafia movie. The face was stronger as well, not the soft expression he'd have when insisting she do her own homework or tossing his favorite quotes out for the hundredth time, but the firm look he showed when she shattered her dinner plate during an argument or screamed about hating her science class. It was an expression she knew wasn't anger. It was, she always thought, a merging of empathy with rigidity. As though he knew what she was feeling and wanted to find a way to make it fit within the bounds he and her mother had set. The scar was there as well, painted as a deep, solid line carved into his chin. As though it were a source of pride for both subject and artist.

She traced the scar, her finger hovering so close

without contact that she thought she could feel the rough surface. She had her own now. Would he even recognize her?

The next portrait, the last in the line, was of an old man. The wrinkles at the sides of his eyes were clear in the fresh paint, maybe only a few years old. There was a kindness under the slight droop of his eyelids. His expression was more that of resignation than confidence. Father Innocent the Fifth, the nameplate indicated. The newest portrait hadn't been completed yet.

The breathing was very clear as Riley approached the opening in the wall facing the portrait. Grunts and groans, metal scrapes, and a hollow step that sounded almost exactly like that of her crutches, only with much more force. She stepped out from where a gap in the weapons wall led to a high-domed, circular interior.

The walls were completely bare. Two openings broke the irregular stone pattern: the one Riley stepped through, and the other fifty feet directly across the circular chamber. In the space between the openings, three figures moved into a triangular formation with each other. The closer two, both of them men, one taller and the other stockier, shuffled their feet against the stone floor, cloaks swinging with movement. They split into a pincer formation around the third figure. They held long swords in both hands in front of them, one man holding it slightly higher on his body while the other tilted the blade to his right. The third figure didn't move, a mass of black cloth crouching low while the larger two moved to flank.

The tall one grunted as he lunged forward. The stockier followed. Their blades flashed with movement. The smaller figure shifted around the taller man, cloak spinning out like a dancer's skirt. There was a metallic tap on the floor. The taller man twisted as the stockier one stuttered his step, his balance slightly off. The tall man reached out to swing weakly. A short blade popped from the smallest fighter's sleeve. The strike was easily parried. The blade disappeared. There was a blur as a single kick knocked the taller man back two steps. The stockier one stumbled trying to get away. The tall man tripped over the stocky one's leg. His sword shook awkwardly as he fell, more afraid of cutting himself than anything else. It was almost pathetic.

Riley heard another metallic echo as the third fighter slid into position in front of the stocky man. He tried to pivot in response. Another kick caught his leg, buckling his weight and dropping the man to the hard ground.

The tall man started to rise. Another spin and the crouched figure was behind him. There was the mechanical click. The short blade appeared across the tall man's throat. "Dead," said a mousy voice from behind the cloth stretched over the face under the hood. The figure jumped over the taller man, tucking into a low somersault that swung the bottom of the cloak out so quickly it slapped the tall man in the chin. The third fighter seemed to shoot through the air, landing in a crouch with one arm out. The blade lingered two inches from the stocky man's neck. "Dead," the voice said once more.

"Again," said the voice from under the hood.

The two men lumbered up from the floor. They sighed, brushed themselves off, and went back into their initial positions next to each other.

A different movement caught Riley's attention.

"Impressive isn't she?" came the gnarled voice from along the circular wall.

Virgil stopped next to her. He turned to watch Sister Dove allow the two recruits to move wherever they pleased, keeping a low crouch the entire time. The cloak masked her small frame, blending it into the floor, hiding her balance points and momentum.

"She does love to play."

"I've never seen anyone like that before," Riley said, eyes glued to where Dove seemed to rise from the floor like water pulling itself up. The two men were already shaking.

"Your father was even better," Virgil said.

Dove didn't move as the two men circled around her, swords drooping with uncertainty.

"His every movement was precise and considered."

Dove giggled.

"He was the greatest I've ever seen."

Riley glanced back to the opening, the wall where her father's portrait hung several feet from her sight. His portrait would be the next. Father Vigilius the Thirteenth, Prior of the Order of the Hidden Blade, said to be chosen by fate itself as the successor of Innocent the Fifth.

There was a whoosh and a grunt as one of the men hit the ground again. Riley turned back to see Dove's arms stretched between the two men, blade pointed at the fallen man's face, sword pointed at the standing man's belly. "Dead," Dove repeated once more.

"I can't imagine it," Riley said.

"Nor could I," Virgil replied, "Until I saw it myself."

"Again," Dove commanded.

"You could be better," Riley heard from above her.

She looked up to see Virgil shifting to stand in front of her. He held one hand calmly over the other. The sleeves of his loose, high-collared shirt reached down to his thumbs. His black pants resembled those her school's basketball team wore during warm-ups. Casual dress, she assumed, worn outside of . . . formal functions. "You are a McKnight," Virgil continued. "It's in your blood."

There was an ache under Riley's arms where she pushed against the crutches. She straightened her back to move the pressure onto her uninjured leg, leaving only a little for the walking cast to support. There was a tingle of pain in her left thigh where the two breaks were still healing. She leaned more to the right.

"Have you come to a decision yet?" Virgil asked, still staring down at her. Riley cast her eyes downward. The stone floor nearly shined, even with the scratches and worn-down textures of age. A man grunted.

"I'm not sure," she said.

"It's a big decision," Virgil replied in his jagged tone. "You're wise to be precise and judicious, like your father was. You would also be wise to understand just how vital our organization has been to your lineage." There were heavy steps on the stones beyond him. A sharp metal smack against the ground. Riley tried leaning around Virgil. "Even your family name," he said, tilting to block her view, "is a testament to your ancestors' involvement." She brought her eyes up to meet his, the lines of his face deep and thin like cracks eroded into canyon walls.

"You are exposed," she heard from behind him.

"This entitles you to certain . . . benefits . . . no other recruits receive."

"Such as?"

Virgil took a step back. "Sister Dove."

"Stop," Dove commanded flatly.

Virgil moved to the side, revealing where the

stocky man had dropped to one knee and hand, breathing heavily, his hood yanked back from his head while the tall man held both arms across his midsection, as though he'd either been hit hard in the stomach or really needed a bathroom break, or both. Dove stood perfectly still and upright in the center of the room. She held one sword in each hand. She was completely black under the hood and behind the cloth stretched across her face.

"Play nice, Sister," Virgil said as Riley crutched behind him through the other opening in the circular wall.

The swords rattled on the stone. "Again," Riley heard from within the room behind her.

A trio of hallways branched out from the other side of the circular chamber. The path to her left continued on until the lantern light faded. She could see a pair of doors of either side of the hallway, then more doors only on one side while weapon racks lined the other. The path to her right looked exactly the same, but without the weapon racks. Virgil continued forward, down the center hall, which likely extended beyond the fenced-in area above them and under the forest. Half a dozen trips to this location and she still had no idea how far it went in any direction.

"She was right around your age," Virgil said, pausing his progress to look back at Riley. The lantern light deepened the slivers extending from his eyes.

"Dove?" Riley asked.

"The girl who was found on the tracks last night. Dawn Musgrave. Did you know her?"

Riley stopped moving. "Dawn?" she said. "I met her but didn't really know her. She was in the class above mine. A bit of a jerk, actually"—she shook her head—"but that doesn't mean she deserved what happened."

"Doesn't it?" Virgil asked. "We all get what we deserve, Riley. Most are merely ignorant of why." He started down the hall again.

"I don't agree," Riley said.

"Fate doesn't care if you agree," Virgil replied.

She stared at his back for a moment. She glanced at the set of casts covering her leg before continuing in his trail. They passed a couple more wooden doors with metal knobs and large keyholes on their way to what Riley had dubbed "the office." Third door on the right, unlocked.

Lanterns hanging in each corner cast dull yellow on the bare walls. Dark patches covered places on the stone as though a painted image had faded a long, long time ago. A large armoire occupied the front half of the left wall. Intricate carvings covered its wide, wooden face. Curves, swirls, and circular patterns were carved into the wood in three layers, crossing over the division in the pair of doors—and yet, somehow, maintaining a balance between the two sides. The piece contrasted sharply with the desk placed near the back of the room, which looked more like a slab of solid rock than a piece of furniture. Four simple wooden chairs crowded around it, three with their backs to the door and one on the other side. She couldn't see it, but the desk must have been cut into for the person on that side to slide their legs under, or Virgil would not have been able to sit as he did with his back straight and his folded hands on the table.

He motioned for Riley to sit in the same chair she had during previous visits. She leaned her crutches against the seatback. The walking cast barely hovered over the ground as she lowered with all her weight on the other leg.

"I trust you have heard the details of this latest incident," he said.

Riley nodded. She recalled the news report she'd seen after meeting Nate earlier that morning, an update on the body found late last night after a teenage boy frantically phoned the police about an attack on him and his girlfriend. They found her a hundred feet from where the tracks crossed over the Lewis Highway, on the other side of town, toward the Annex Lakes.

"And you know what was responsible," Virgil said.

There weren't many details in the report. Nothing about possible suspects or motives. The report cut to a police officer saying that the body was "nearly decapitated" and the boy was "in considerable shock."

"Sounds like a bear," Riley said.

Virgil stared at her. He sat perfectly still. He didn't even seem to breathe. Riley looked to the dimly lit room around them. "This tragedy was no more a work of nature than your accident was." He stared at her. "I believe you know this as well."

"I don't know anything anymore," she said. "It happened so fast that I couldn't see anything. One second we were heading home and next we were swerving and upside down and . . . " She took a breath. "And that was all."

Virgil turned away. Shadows moved across his face from sunrise to sunset.

Riley furrowed her brow at him.

"No." He shook his head.

"No what?" she replied.

Virgil turned toward her again, the lights firing in his eyes. "No, you can't remain so blind as to deny what you know is happening. Not you." The echo in the small room made his voice an avalanche. "Not with your lineage and experience."

"I don't see what my lineage has to do with this."

"You, Riley McKnight, are one of us. You may not have been aware of it before, but you can't say you don't feel a connection now."

It was Riley who shook her head this time, snorting a laugh.

"This is your path, McKnight. Deny it now if you wish, but eventually you will come to understand what must be done."

"And what is that, exactly?" Riley snapped. "Hunt werewolves? And what's after that? Are we going to ride unicorns into a battle against Dracula and a rabid Easter Bunny?"

Virgil titled his head back to look at her. She

returned his stare, trying not to let him see the quiver in her jaw or the moisture gathering in her eyes.

"If you refuse to believe, then why do you insist on returning here?"

Riley rubbed at the cast over her leg, behind the desk where she assumed Virgil couldn't see. She felt two stings of pain in her thigh. The scars on her face matched the wrinkles on his, deep lines carved from living too long. She saw her blood dripping onto the fabric of the vehicle ceiling below.

"You say you can make me better," she said quietly.

"Yes," Virgil replied, nodding, "you can become better than you ever hoped. But not like this. Not without a commitment. Not without belief."

Riley turned away once more. Her fingers pressed the pad over her leg.

"Perhaps I was wrong about you, Riley." She glanced up as Virgil said this. "Perhaps you can't be anything more than what you are now . . ."

She narrowed her eyes at him.

" . . . A broken little girl."

Her jaw flexed. Her nostrils flared.

"Should I send for someone to help you up the stairs?"

"Screw you!" Riley shouted.

He waved two fingers at her in dismissal.

Riley turned in her chair to pull the crutches to her side. "Crazy old jerk," she said, covering the effort of pushing up from the hard wood chair onto one leg and to the crutches. She took a moment to wipe at her eyes before swinging her legs toward the door.

"We have much to offer you here," the gravelly voice said, "but we demand much as well."

The hollow metallic sound followed her out the door.

"One day you will understand," the voice continued. "I pray it won't be too late."

CHAPTER 4

THE FAT LADY GROANED AS HER LEG SLOWLY rose into the air. The muscular trainer, Will, pressed down on her knee as he pushed her ankle up from the massage table along the wall of the clinic. The foot froze in the air, far from straight up. Riley couldn't even do that anymore, not without intense pain shooting through her entire leg. Might never be able to do that again. She felt the phone vibrate in her pocket. Text message from Mom: I'm here.

Riley yanked the door hard enough that she heard the blinds over the window rattle. She extended her crutches so far that she had to drag her foot to keep from kicking the car at the end of the curb.

"How was it?" her mother asked as soon as the back door opened.

"Fine," Riley answered, laying the two metal poles on the backseat. She slammed the door shut, took one hop, and opened the passenger side.

"Progressing?"

"I'm not sure." She tossed her backpack into the footwell. She'd wetted her bathing suit and wrapped it in the towel in her bag to make it seem like she'd gone swimming instead of to the forest. She dropped into the seat, trying not to wince from the impact.

"Don't worry, hon," her mom assured, "you'll get back to normal soon."

Riley snorted a laugh.

Riley took a deep breath as she turned the corner

of the landing between the second and third floor in her apartment building. She held both crutches under one arm. It wasn't difficult to hop up the three floors to her apartment, but the impact of landing would vibrate through her leg just enough to sting.

"You know this is why the building has an elevator," her mother said from a few steps behind her.

"It's only three floors," Riley replied as she started up the last set of stairs.

"Just don't strain yourself, hon."

She gave a final push to clear the last two steps in one jump.

"The last thing you need is to reinjure yourself now."

"It's a more efficient use of energy," Riley replied as she swung the crutches out and around to her sides.

"Is that what Diane told you?"

Riley leaned far into the first step, swinging with

such force that it felt as though her legs could go parallel to the floor.

"I'm sure it isn't," her mother answered.

The crutches shook against Riley's arms. The muffled metal taps on the floor alternated with the light sole of her shoe: heavy-soft, heavy-soft. Each step louder than Dove's, even as she had spun around and sprang through the air. Riley pounded the crutches down and thrust her legs forward.

"Any dinner requests?" her mom asked, giving Riley plenty of room to move.

"Not really."

"Does Diane have any diet tips? Like milk for bone growth or protein for muscle retention?"

Riley shook her head.

"Hmmm?" her mother prompted.

"No."

"Okay. Spaghetti sound good?"

"That's fine," Riley replied.

"Maybe I'll just see what we already have."

"That's fine too."

"Or maybe we'll just snack on that chip on your shoulder," her mother muttered.

Riley stopped a step away from the front door of their apartment at the corner of the building. Her mother dug through her pocket for the keys. She paused before opening the door.

"Are you okay?" she asked, the tiredness in her face coming through in the late afternoon sun high in the window.

Riley shook her head as she turned away. "I'm . . . tired of needing these," she said, shrugging the crutches up and down. "Things used to be so much easier."

"I hate to tell you this, dear," her mother said with a slight smile, "but you'll say that many times in your life." She pushed the door open. She held it for Riley to crutch in. "Luckily, you'll live a long time, so this"—she motioned toward the casts—"will be a short inconvenience before you're fixed right up. Just don't rush it."

Riley circled around into the living room of the

85

apartment. She leaned to see through the opening into the kitchen. The window on the corner looked down on the bank across the street. Virgil didn't dig through the trash cans there anymore.

"Sure," Riley muttered, "fixed right up."

Some stupid old sitcom was on the television when she turned it on while she started pulling apart the Velcro straps that held her cast in place. Each pull was a flash of television static, a shot of white noise. Like a break. Sudden. Like glass. She shook the thought away as she stretched forward, bending her knee, to press the button that released one pole connecting the two casts together. She moved the boot enough that she could release the other side without much effort. She felt the pressure in the back of her leg and shoulders as she stretched over herself to pull the boot off, bending her knee even more to reach.

She couldn't keep her leg straight any more than the fat lady on the table could keep her's.

She wondered how other people accomplished removing this device themselves. At least she didn't need help lying down or going to the bathroom. She wasn't that broken.

The knee piece was the easiest: release the catches, slide out, and pull away.

She closed her eyes before starting on the cast over her thigh. It wasn't as difficult, since she only needed to open the straps and the padding over the top, but there were slight twitches and turns that shot pain through her whole leg if she wasn't careful.

"That's what they call me," said the television to a fit of simulated laughter.

Riley gritted her teeth as she pulled the first of the four straps open. Another shot of static. A tiny shatter. Then another and another and another. There was a knock on the door.

"Sweetie," Riley's mother said from outside, "I'm

heading out to get pasta for spaghetti, anything you need?"

"Nothing," Riley called back to her mom. "Nothing you could get me anyway," she added to herself.

There was a quick stab in her upper thigh as Riley took the plastic frame from the internal padding. She cringed through it. Several quick yanks opened the covering, exposing her broken leg. It looked even lighter than usual, indentations from where the frame and straps squeezed through the pad. She couldn't see it, but she knew there was a brutal scar running almost the entire back of her leg. *Broken little girl,* she heard again, the voice like rocks falling in her head.

She gritted her teeth as she lifted her leg to stuff a pillow beneath the thigh. The hurt lingered after releasing the muscles but didn't feel like she'd done anything wrong. She slid forward on the bed until her body was low enough that the thigh was angled above her head. That was how she had to be now, anytime she wasn't on her feet. Even sitting was still only for special occasions. Like awkward visits with friends or being insulted by old men who hunted werewolves in their spare time. Or was that a full-time gig? No wonder he looked homeless.

The weird-looking blond lady on the television rolled her eyes at the oddly handsome man with the big chin. "Hey, I'm not judging," he said to more laughter. Riley searched around for the remote. It sat at the foot of the bed.

"Not worth it," she groaned.

Her eyes caught on the open closet door. The sleeves of all her coats and jackets spilled out from the frame. She left other items piled on the floor of the closet: the faded junior high gymnastics sweater she'd worn around the apartment the last couple of days and the blue sweatpants with the left leg chopped off.

She ran her fingers over the three streaks of tough skin cut into her face, then tapped the smaller dents.

Toward the back of her closet, right next to the

wall, behind the long red overcoat she'd worn once but felt insecure about and the blue- and gray-striped flannel she'd thought was cool for about a week, a dark green sleeve extended lower than the others. She remembered the old grease and cigarette smells of the thing. They were probably gone by now, those scents, replaced by dust or drywall or laundry detergent, but they remained in her memory. Not like she was ever going to forget.

That jacket. She'd worn it so much it had become a part of how people knew her. Then: the girl with the strong legs, the Army jacket, and the dead father. Now: the girl with the broken leg, the dead father, and the scarred face. And the dead boyfriend. She was even less than she'd been all those years before.

Riley knocked her head against the pillow.

Broken little girl.

She closed her eyes.

Nothing to fix her right up.

She opened her eyes, blinking the tears out.

The words dropped on her like a cave-in.

*Can't be anything more than what you are now.
Broken little girl.*

CHAPTER 5

It didn't look late when Nate arrived home, with the summer sun still an hour from setting. But ten o'clock was later than expected after he'd commandeered his mother's truck with only a vague "Riley needs a ride to PT."

As much as he hated lying to his mom, it wasn't as though she hadn't done the exact same thing to him for years. For his entire life, in fact. She could have called him anytime if she wanted, so she probably already guessed where he was. He was learning all the things she had lied to him about. So technically it was her fault he was late, and her fault he lied to her.

She was on the couch when he entered. A sitcom was on the television, the bland colors, blurred lines, and overbearing laugh track marked it as several years old. It was the type of mindless thing she'd watch when she was cleaning or reading or having difficulties keeping herself from changing. Background noise, line, line, laugh, line, line, laugh. Every joke choreographed and safe. Nothing unexpected. Nothing at all like real life. Whatever "real life" was these days.

"Hey," Nate's mother said, her focus remaining on the television. The mechanical crowd hooted at some remark from the blond lady with her arms folded. "How's Riley?"

"She's . . . " He thought for a moment about how to respond. Riley seemed distant, but that might've been him. She was talking but what was he supposed to say? How was he supposed to act around her after what happened, what he knew, what he was? Anytime he even *tried* to look at her, all he saw were the three scars he'd scratched into the side of her face. He wanted to help her, but instead, he'd hurt her even more. All because he'd been hunted over what he was, what he'd never known about himself . . . what he could never tell her. Was there a way he was "supposed to act" in those cases?

"Fine," he answered after what he feared had been too long in silence. "Her doctor said she's recovering well."

"You were with her this whole time?" his mother asked. There was more laughter from the television as the dopey guy said something dopey.

"Pretty much," he replied.

"How's her movement?" She turned toward him just before the show cut to a commercial.

"Good enough, considering she's on crutches again."

His mom attempted a sympathetic smile, "At least she's had some practice with those."

"Yeah," Nate replied. He lowered his head and took a step toward the stairs up to his room.

"How are you with all this?"

"I'm fine," he said without stopping.

"I'm fine," she mimicked. "You expect me to believe that?"

He stopped, exhaling heavily.

"It was awkward, wasn't it, seeing her like that?"

The way Riley had sat, uneasily shifted to one side . . . He knew it was from the fractures in her legs. If she'd sat that way because she'd known what he was, she would have reacted much differently. She would have remained hidden behind her building door, the way the nurse had that night. She would have called the police like the receptionist, or kept her distance like the security guard.

She'd said he hadn't been there. Had told him he couldn't have protected her and didn't have control of what had happened. He hadn't even been able to look at her as she spoke. That might have been a mistake. Did he normally look at people as they scolded him? He'd scowled at Maier, but Maier wasn't Riley. He and Maier had never promised to not do anything bad to each other.

"Did you have dinner while you were out?" Nate's mother asked, moving on.

"Not really."

"I made some chili a couple hours ago. It's in the fridge if you want it."

"I'm okay," Nate said. The laughter returned.

"C'mon," his mother said, "I'll heat some up for you." He heard a muffled tap on the couch cushion. He turned to see her already moving around the armrest. "You want a salad?"

"No thanks."

"I'll make a little one for you." She stopped a foot away from where the living room carpet ended and the kitchen tiles began. There was a slight redness to her eyes, a puff in the skin beneath them. She gestured toward the couch again. "C'mon, have a seat. It'll just take a couple of minutes."

Nate shrugged.

"That's the spirit," his mother said as she stepped into the kitchen.

"Are you okay?" he asked, turning as she passed.

"Been better but . . . you know," she said before disappearing behind the kitchen wall.

Nate shuffled around to the other side of the couch, opposite from where his mother had been sitting. He could hear her opening the refrigerator door, the *ting* of the metal bowl on the kitchen counter. "You can change that if you want," she called from the kitchen over the sound of the large knife being laid on the cutting board. The sexy blond lady, the sexy brunette lady, and the dopey guy were having a conversation while seated around one table at a coffee shop. The chairs were arranged so that they barely saw each other as they spoke, playing instead to the camera in front of them. Talking that way wasn't strange for them.

He was barely facing his mother now too, as he had with Riley. Withholding once again, as he had with Riley. He couldn't look either of them in the face. Maybe that was his tell.

The dopey guy said something which made the blond lady roll her eyes. The brunette replied, "That's what she said," a comeback apparently so clever and unexpected that the crowd was programmed to roar with approval. In the background, Nate could hear the knife on the cutting board and the hum of the microwave. That's what it all was: background noise. Better than letting your thoughts fill the silence. The microwave dinged.

"You want a soda or anything?" his mom called out as she opened the microwave.

"Sure," he replied, trying to sound more open.

"Well, you need to get that yourself. I've already done my motherly duties for the evening." The canned crowd seemed to find his mother quite funny.

Nate made sure to look at his mother as they passed each other near where the living room carpet met the kitchen tile. She smiled at him, both of her hands placed carefully beneath a hot pad cradling the dark blue bowl they'd had since before he could remember. There used to be two others. He dropped one and the other disappeared as though it never existed. "Grab the salad as well as any dressing you might want from the fridge," his mom said after placing the bowl on the coffee table between the couch and the television mounted on the wall.

Nate grabbed a can from the fridge. He circled around to the small white bowl of vegetables on the kitchen counter. "So what did you do all day?" he heard from the other room.

"Movies, talked, the usual," he answered without hesitation.

"Which movies did you watch?"

"We did a *Toy Story* marathon. Nothing too heavy. She'd never seen the second one." He turned to cross into the living room.

"You might want a fork, as well," his mother said as though on cue. He could almost hear the laugh track coming in.

"Did she like it?" she asked, trolling for information.

"I think so," he said, trying to sound as natural as possible, unlike the characters on the television, just in case his previous hesitance hadn't given him away. "She fell asleep a couple of times though, PT and all."

She was looking over the back of the couch when he stepped into the living room.

"How's her mom?"

"She was at work."

She raised her eyebrow at him. "Until ten?"

He felt her stare following as he walked around the other side of the couch, placed the drink and salad down next to the steaming chili, and dropped onto the cushion farthest away from her.

He sat still a moment, watching the steam rise from the bowl in front of him. Earlier that day he would have seen the scent of it, steaming all the same. That was how they "saw" the world, through their sense of smell. It was better than sight. They could see things hundreds of feet away, even through other objects. Smell was everywhere.

Ulrich had told him this. His mother never had.

He glanced over to her at the other side of the couch. She leaned back in the corner, feet up and knees bent, arms folded over her chest. He looked away. He hated lying to her anyway.

"They say you tried to deny me my birthright."

He heard her huff.

"That my foolishness is what got that girl killed this morning."

"Who says that?"

"Councilor Maier."

She scoffed. "Of course it would be him."

"He says that if I'd known what I was before, then maybe the incident wouldn't have happened. The chase and Riley's . . . accident."

She shook her head with her arms still crossed, fuming.

"Maier thinks because I nearly exposed myself

that the Order will use this opportunity to frame us and provoke action."

"Maier was spouting that garbage even before I joined that damn council," his mother finally said, pushing out of the corner of the couch. Her legs folded in front of her. "To him everything is a plot to expose us, or a slight against our kind, or a planned assault on our existence."

She shook her head, crossing her arms again.

"He says that if Dad were alive then none of this would have happened."

His mother chuckled at that. He could see the shadows in her jaws rise, as they had in the hospital when he woke up after his first change.

"Maybe if I had known before," Nate said, trying to sound more contemplative than accusatory.

"Fine!" She threw her hands out once again. "He's right! They were all right!"

He turned away. He slouched with his elbows on his knees.

"I should have told you. Is that what you want to hear?"

The steam had faded from the blue bowl.

"So if you want to blame someone then it may as well be me."

Nate closed his eyes. He imagined her sitting with her arms and legs crossed on the other side of the couch. She'd shake her head and flex her jaw. There may even be that familiar heat growing inside her chest.

"It was my decision not to tell you when I should have long ago. If someone has to be beaten up for what happened, then okay, I'll take it."

He opened his eyes again. He straightened up. It felt better to keep his back rigid. It was more confident, more civilized.

"You had your reasons," he said.

"That's right." He felt the couch shift as she leaned forward. "May not have been the best decision, but it was my choice. It was what I thought was best at the time."

He remained upright. He didn't turn toward her.

"After everything I went through. I couldn't do that again."

He took a deep breath. He let it leak out slowly. Like steam.

"We can't know how things are going to end."

He couldn't help slouching once more. He put his elbows on his knees and his head against his hands. It was more hidden, less civilized. It felt appropriate.

"We can only try the best we can at the time."

"I know, Mom," he said with his head down.

"Good," she said, "Then I'll trust you to do whatever you think is best."

He felt the couch shift again as she stood up.

"Even if that means blaming all your misfortunes on me."

He heard her stomp around the couch and toward her room.

"I deserve it all."

The door creaked open.

"Don't forget to clean up when you're done."

The door slammed.

The audience laughed.

CHAPTER 6

Night was good. Better than the day. In the night there was no expectation of being able to see. It helped Nate transition from the human dependency on sight to experiencing the world through smell. Distance was a concentration of scent, from the bark and mold outside of a tree trunk, to the dirt and grass on the ground, to any other animals in the forest.

Nate felt the power behind every push of the huge muscles in his legs. It felt good. He zigzagged between the tall trees of the nature preserve without having to slow down. He leapt right and left easily, the drawstring bag he put over his shoulders tilting with each movement. The strings were tight but didn't stretch to breaking as he feared they would after the change. He bounced off his hands and the rough skin covering his palms. He felt the spring in his kicks off the ground. He ran through the forest faster than he remembered ever driving down the road which divided it. He felt safer this way, in the dark, among the scents he could see well in every direction.

He didn't have to think about where he was going, he knew where everything was, their odors registering in his mind unconsciously, smoke columns disappearing into the distance behind him before he truly noticed they were there. He didn't need to know exactly where things were. Awareness was enough. Go where other objects were not. And above everything else, don't be seen. Not again.

A presence of concrete, grease, oil, sweat, paper, garbage—humanity—rose from beyond those of leaves and dirt and moss and dew. He stayed on the outskirts of the town rather than heading straight for it. He couldn't make that mistake again. Not with the hell it raised last time. Another sighting would only make Maier rattle off even more insults about him and his mom. He'd probably have to apologize to her at some point, although . . . why? What did he have to apologize for other than not being told the truth about himself? The incident, the Council, Maier, his awkwardness with Riley, they were all based off that. But he didn't want his mom to feel bad either. She did her best.

Dealing with other people, be they like him or not, that was the problem. This part—speeding through a dark forest, feeling his own power, *seeing* everything within hundreds of feet in all directions—this was the good part. He wanted to enjoy this. Too bad it would so quickly be over.

He stayed in the forest as he changed back. He gritted his teeth as his body pulled into itself, his animalistic fur somehow disappearing into his skin. He imagined his bones like a collapsible telescope pushing into itself, except with living parts instead of metal. He shook as the pain ripped through his body, feeling more concentrated as he grew smaller. Every inch of muscle and skin throbbed. He dropped to his knees at the base of a large tree. He propped himself up against the trunk, the rough bark poking the soft skin of his palm. He closed his eyes. He groaned into a roar.

Then it was over. His left shoulder and the back of his legs twitched like aftershocks following a tremor, but the pain was gone. He was normal again . . . for lack of a more accurate term. Normal and human and bent forward with one hand holding him up against a tree, on his knees, and naked. The drawstring bag sagged to his lower back. It almost reached the ground.

Complete black greeted him as he opened his eyes. He blinked several times quickly. There was a light scent of the forest, but that was it. Forest. Nothing more specific than that. He saw a couple of distant streetlights filtering through the leaves, very slight variation in the trees in front of him, and that was all. From sensing everything to sensing nothing. It's a wonder humanity made it so far with such a limited scope.

He got dressed before going any farther. A pair of faded jeans that were always a bit too big for him, a black sweatshirt with NOT ALL WHO WANDER ARE LOST written over an image of a pair of hiking boots, and the old shoes that his mother brought him when he was in the hospital after the first time he'd changed. At least he was prepared this time, and not bowing on the floor of a waiting room, mooning anyone who looked inside. It wasn't the kind of exposure Maier and his group had been complaining about, but it was almost as embarrassing.

He peaked out from the trees on the border of the clearing before the town. He stayed in the trees until he reached the gap in the fence behind the houses at the edge of the road. It would be slower travel from here but shouldn't take more than fifteen minutes to reach the museum in the center of the southern part of town. He instinctively checked for his phone but found only house keys and the museum card he'd packed before leaving. Probably should have brought the phone as well, or a watch at least. *Next time.* He'd also probably bring a light jacket or a thicker shirt, clothes that would keep away the chill once his fur coat was gone.

Nate crossed the last street before the museum. He stopped at the tall fence dividing the museum from the shops next door with a pair of gates blocking entry. The alley was big enough for delivery vans to enter. He checked out the road. Thin streetlights shined white-yellow circles on the sidewalk. A chain securing a newspaper box to a lamppost clinked as it swayed in the breeze. Nate had a sudden image of Virgil standing over the trash can on the other side of the light, his thinning hair reflecting white. He wasn't there. No one was there.

Nate glanced up at the security camera positioned at the corner of the building. The guards always let him pass before without question. It seemed like the entire museum staff was filled with them. *His people.* How many were there?

He looked up at the gate, about seven feet high with a thick chain and a big lock. The links were smooth and nearly glittered at him when he leaned closer. Signs attached to the fence with thin wires told him to "KEEP OUT" and that the alley was "MUSEUM PROPERTY. TRESPASSERS WILL BE PROSECUTED." He looked at the camera again, twelve feet up on the wall and faced directly at him. The red light on the side reminded him of the laser scope used in some action movies. He half expected to see a red dot on himself. Back to the gate.

He imagined leaping over the entire thing in his wolf form. He'd done something like it before, leaping the fence on the edge of the forest as he raced to the hospital. But changing in town would be a mistake. The pain of the change, feeling his bones stretch and the hair push out as though sewing pins were being stuck from the inside of his skin, it would be hard to contain his groans and growls. He'd done enough of that already. Nate looked at the camera yet again. The single *Terminator* eye stared back. The gate shook with a soft clank as he took hold of the chain.

He pulled himself up slowly to not rock back and forth. He checked over his shoulder, watching for movement on the street or in the windows of the building across. It would be so much easier in changed form. Not only could he leap over the fence, but he would know exactly where everyone was, where they were going, and if they were reacting to him or not. He imagined their adrenaline would spike a bit seeing this huge, fur-covered beast bounding over the back gate into the Natural History Museum.

The thin metal in his hands reminded him of when he and Riley would occasionally hop fences onto hiking trails. He was all right, a couple of steps up, over, a step down, and jump to the ground. It was as though Riley practiced. She'd be up, over, and down before he'd get his second leg to the other side. At least, that's how she used to be. No telling if she'd be such a good fence climber anymore. Or if she'd be inclined to climb fences at all. The impact in his legs made him miss having ropey muscles and thick bones absorbing the shock of bounding through the forest.

He walked down the alley before reaching the loading zone for the museum, near the rear of the B gallery. Another camera watched as he approached the large doors of the entrance. The red dot blinked instead of steadily shining. He pressed his card on the small black box on the wall. He gently pushed the long bar across the door. No light came from inside.

Nate traced the wall with one hand. He saw the shadows of the path leading toward the intersection of the second gallery. The lighter black of the pictures on these walls reminded him of the posters in his room or the photos lining the stairs in his house. He assumed his mother had gone to sleep before he left, but maybe she hadn't. Would she be angry to find out he'd left? He saw the dark shadow of the door ahead. He leaned in close to see the frame of the door, the lighter color of the metallic handle, and the darker black of the keycard lock. He guessed at which side of the card to hold against the box. He guessed again, pressed the handle down. Light emerged as he pushed the door open.

"—get there, check it out, and leave." A woman's voice bounced off the drawers in the hall.

There was a low growl that rumbled behind it.

"We're going to investigate and nothing more, you got it?"

There was another voice which Nate couldn't quite understand. It was low and raspy. At once both sharp and rounded, hissy and brutish.

"You're late," the woman said.

He saw the shadows in the main chamber move over the ground ahead. A dark woman with strong features peeked through the gap. It took Nate a moment to register this woman as the same one he'd seen in the school's parking lot the afternoon before Riley's crash. The one who'd switched from determined to stuttering for no apparent reason.

"S-Sorry," Nate said, still puzzling over the presence of the woman. Was the man with her again? "Didn't know how long it would take to run here."

There was a snarled, rolling exhale like a beastly sigh.

The wolf came into view as Nate neared. It was the same beast he'd seen earlier that day, or the day before since it was now past one in the morning, with the bushy chin hair and the pointed fur running up its head and along its shoulders. The wolf stared at Nate through tiny black dots in the center of bright red eyes.

"Did you see anyone on the way here?" the woman asked.

Nate shook his head.

"Did anyone see you?"

"Not that I know of."

She squinted at this a moment. "Did Ulrich tell you what we're doing here?"

"We're looking for things the police would've missed."

"Right," she said. "Scents, tracks, blood, viscera, shoe scuffs, grease, anything that people wouldn't have been able to see." She glanced around at the others. Nate was surprised again to see Mr. Clarkson leaning against the wall on the near side of the room. He didn't have the square glasses he'd wear at school or during the previous meeting. "It's been a full day since the attack so we need to be thorough. Captain Reynolds has cleared a window between patrols but we also need to be quick." She looked at each of them. Clarkson nodded. He carried a laptop bag which reached his knee. The wolf glared through blood-tinted eyes. "Got it?" she asked, looking at Nate.

He nodded.

She took a step toward the wolf. Her model-like

height still left her a full foot shorter than he was while slouched.

"Just because Maier insists you come along doesn't give you permission to do anything but observe. Understand?"

The wolf's lips and jaw barely moved, like someone with a broken jaw trying to speak. Its response rolled together into a short sound which Nate couldn't figure out.

"You could have brought some clothes with you at least," she muttered.

The wolf curled his lip in response.

"That means whatever happens," the woman said, her commanding tone returning as her view moved between the three of them, "you listen to me. No matter what."

Clarkson nodded once more. Nate followed his lead.

"Nathaniel," the woman said, turning directly to him. Her straightened posture made her nearly as tall as he was. "Recite the Code of the Blood for us."

The lines came immediately to mind, forced into memory the same way the photos along the stairs in his house had been: repetition and habit, but in a much shorter time.

"We of the blood shall never harm a human," he said, "We of the blood shall never harm another of the blood." The woman nodded as he listed each item. "We of the blood shall never use our gifts for personal gain. None but those of the blood shall know we exist."

The woman spun toward the others.

"There are some who believe that the Order has broken our Accord." She glanced at the wolf. "This claim requires evidence." Her gaze moved across Clarkson and landed on Nate. "For the sake of peace, I hope we find nothing."

The wolf snorted.

"Councilor Clarkson, I'd like you to accompany Mr. Zarker."

"Are you sure?" Clarkson asked.

"Ulrich insisted that I keep an eye on the pup

myself." She moved a step closer as though to whisper. "We're both babysitters on this run," she said no quieter than before.

Clarkson smiled lightly. "Yes, Lady Shayera."

She stepped away once more. "You two head north and stick to the trees. We'll meet you at the scene."

The wolf grunted. His whole, massive body seemed to ripple as he kicked into motion. Nate moved to let him pass. He watched as the wolf had to twist slightly to fit between the drawers lining the hallway.

"How are you doing with all this?" Clarkson spoke quietly, leaning in.

"I'm . . . adjusting."

"And how about with Riley?"

"She seems to be recovering," Nate said.

Clarkson looked confused for a moment, almost as though Nate had answered the wrong question. "See you out there," he said before stepping away.

Nate turned toward the only other person left in the room. The woman, Shayera, blinked away.

"Ummm . . . " she said, "That— that day in the parking lot," she sputtered, as though someone had sapped all of her confidence in a second. "Zarker and I heard you were at the school and thought that your mother would have—" She shook her head as though resetting. She took a breath.

"Zarker . . . " Nate wondered. "That was the same guy—"

"It wasn't our place," she blurted, glancing at him and then down, eyes twitching nearly as much as Dustin Hoffman in *Rain Man*. "We just . . . we wanted to say hello is all."

The demure stance didn't fit the broad shoulders and the toned collarbone visible above the tank top under the black leather jacket, or the strong cheekbones, chin, and nose that the light seemed to stroll upon.

"Are you okay?" Nate said at last.

Shayera took a breath. She lifted her chin.

"Your father was a great man," she said quick and flat. "And even though your mother chose a different path for herself, I have always admired her strength."

"Ummm," Nate said as Shayera lowered her eyes again, more in reverence than in insecurity. "Thanks."

"Sorry for that other time," she said without turning away. "Also sorry about what happened to your friend. We were all . . . surprised to hear of her involvement."

Nate furrowed his brow at this.

"So," Shayera said, reaching for a square knapsack on the ground. She looked up at him as though the switch in her head had shifted back to confident. "After you," she said, motioning toward the hall.

"You're the leader here," Nate replied. "I'll follow you."

"No," she said, confidence rising in her voice. Her features suddenly solid in the light. "You're the leader here."

"What do you—"

"Please," she said, gesturing toward the hallway again. "After you."

CHAPTER 7

Police barricades separated the road from the murder scene. It took a second for that term to kick in. Murder scene. Someone had died here. Someone around Nate's age, who'd attended Nate's school, who'd walked into and out of the same classes. Someone who'd taken the climb just as often as he did. The idea only became concrete once they arrived, as the blood stung the deep channels of his snout. Traces of sweat mixed with iron from both the tracks and the blood spilled on them.

The blood was expected, as was the dirt and steel, trees, grass, moss, and the musk of the others with him. The largest of them, Zarker, had a particularly powerful odor, as though years of grease and dead skin had been smeared into the fur covering his body, creating a heavy yellow-orange hue that permeated the air around him. Shayera and Clarkson were a less-intense yellow, the hot color of animal life, but a calmer color than the blazing red of danger. Seeing the world in this way reminded him of infrared sequences in movies, or how the Predator looked at Arnold during their own encounter in the forest. Except, for Nate, it indicated density instead of heat, a difference which seemed to give Zarker a dotted outline, as the dirt and oils came into clumps which built into points in his hair. He was a constellation stalking with sudden movements across the tracks and toward the trees.

Of course, Nate had yet to see what he looked like in this new, altered form, whether through scent or by sight in a mirror or photograph, as Ulrich had advised him to do. It was important to understand how the world would see him, Ulrich claimed, to feel the shock others would. Nate had practiced changing, familiarizing himself with the searing pains that came with stretching bones, hardening skin, and sprouting coarse hairs over his entire body, but he had yet to see himself. He had an expectation of how he looked. To see something else would be a shock. It would be too much. Luckily, the only ones who would see him that way were those like him. That was the fourth rule. Still, it was little wonder those who weren't like him would be frightened. If he couldn't handle looking at himself, then how could anyone else?

Dirt and steel. Trees, grass, and moss. Blood and the musk of the others. Not much else was left on the scene once Nate and Shayera arrived. More than a day later, in the open, on a rail line which still ran a few times per month and cut an alley into the woods where wind howled through. It would have been a miracle if any scent remained in those circumstances. Still, there they were, four hulking beasts, sniffing around as though one of them would suddenly find something no one else could.

Nate took a moment to listen to the leaves shaking, the branches creaking, the wind passing through the hair along the tips of his pointed ears. Red traces still lingered on the tracks and the woods they'd cut through, though it had faded since the investigations hours before. The blood was a minor presence as well, old and still, a dark red as though being absorbed into the lifeless metal and rock.

Nate returned to sniffing about the tracks. A dull stream of metal, rust, burned oil, powdered gravel, and splintered wood was punctuated by drops of dried sweat, likely from the earlier investigation, and the very rare spot of blood dripped from whatever it was that killed Dawn Musgrave.

There was a hiss from near the trees. "Stop."

Nate understood the word clearly. He instinctively inhaled the air for anything in that direction. Zarker stood at the very edge of the forest. A few animal smells wafted in the distance, birds and a pair of rodents.

"What is it?" asked Shayera. Her words were less snarled and slurred than Zarker's.

"Quiet," he snapped. He crouched as he stepped into the first row of dimly smoking blue-gray trees. A dusty scent spiraled behind him.

"There," Zarker said, the center of his form taking on a greater degree of orange than previously. It was a sign of aggression. "Blackrobes."

A rustle came through the trees on the other side of the tracks.

Zarker wheeled around quickly. Nate could smell the adrenaline in Zarker's body, growing redder as he moved to confront the sound. Nate smelled his own adrenaline growing as well.

"Hold," Shayera said. Her voice was sharper than his, more a snare than a bass.

A lone face revealed itself at the edge of the trees, levitating and glowing orange like a haunted house jack-o'-lantern. Nate didn't recognize him. The figure uttered something that Nate couldn't quite understand.

Zarker growled.

There was a shuffle as a pair of hands appeared from under gloves tucked into long sleeves. The hands spread up and out. A hint of metal and leather appeared on the right wrist.

Shayera repeated the same words. They sounded like "Packs of biscuits."

Nate noticed Clarkson moving vaguely toward the other side of the tracks as more rustling came from both sides. He too had taken on a greater reddish color. Shayera remained cooler, a solid orange, calmer than the others. Could the humans see them that way as well?

Zarker growled a low, rumbling warning.

"We are with the Council," Shayera said, slow and clear, enunciating as best she could through lips that weren't made for speech. "Checking the murder scene."

"As are we," said the glowing face and hands.

Zarker remained crouched and prepared, the cocked hammer of a pistol.

"No evidence of Fenrei," Shayera said, the last word sounded as though it rolled easily through her mouth.

"According to the police reports that seems to be the case," the man said, "but we both know that's not the whole story." His voice was measured in the same way that his scent remained steady. A tinge of fear dotted his forehead, lips, and palms, but otherwise he was calm.

A gust of wind shook the leaves. It sounded like applause. Cool, natural scents spiraled around. There was no blinding beacon in the trees. No Virgil near. Or if he was, he didn't want to be seen this time any more than the others, who Nate could hear shuffling in the grass fifty feet farther into the forest.

"If this is one of us, the Council will handle it."

"We have every confidence you will," the man replied.

Zarker growled as his head swayed from one side

of the tracks to the other. "We are merely here to observe," said the calm, glowing face, "as has been our duty for generations."

"Who is *we*?"

"My brothers and sister." The man held his hand wider.

Hoods and masks were pulled away as more faces appeared. Four behind the man and three on the other side of the tracks. They were glowing spots of yellow-orange with hints of dull red. Cautious but not aggressive.

"We will honor the Accord," said Shayera.

"As will we."

A new scent emerged from beyond the others. It pulsed in Nate's mind.

"What is your name, brother?"

The glowing red face drew closer.

"Boniface the Sixth," the man said.

Nate didn't turn from where the first man, Boniface, had appeared in the trees, yet he and the others around him fell away as his focus came upon the face far back from the others.

"And you are Shayera, the Shadow." Boniface's head shifted. "And Zarker, the Wild."

Under their conversation, the wind rustling the leaves, the shuffle of the grass, Zarker's growled breaths, Nate could hear the approach.

"The others, I'm not familiar with."

A hollow echo vibrated through every other footstep.

"Brother Boniface, the High Councilor has ordered us to inspect this scene."

A thick trail followed Dove's burning face as she stepped behind and around the trees. She passed the others with their calm scents. She didn't rush. Her smell didn't even offer a hint of aggression or caution. Still, she glowed in his mind as the bright red of a single stoplight on an empty road, growing large as it neared.

"And our abbot has ordered us to make sure you do not tamper with it," Boniface replied.

He heard Riley in each of Dove's heavy steps. It was the echo of hollow metal used when the legs no longer work. The sound became that of crunching impacts, torn sheet metal, shattered glass. The trail of Dove's red skull was the glow of Remy's brake lights on the trees lining the road.

"We are not here to tamper," Shayera said. "We are here as allies, to learn."

The memory of Dove's piercing, mechanical laughter felt like nails in Nate's head.

"You claim to be allies," Boniface replied, "yet you come prepared for battle."

"We come prepared to see for ourselves," said Shayera, a hint of annoyance in her tone, "the way no one else can."

"And the same is true for us." Boniface appeared calmer than ever.

Nate turned just as Dove neared the edge of the forest. Stabbing pains enclosed his fingertips as razors emerged from the top, pushing the skin up as they grew longer and thicker. His growl rolled out under his breath. He sensed a sudden spike in Shayera's heart rate, a shot of red in her.

Dove's steps went all but silent on the dirt separating trees and tracks.

"Councilor," Shayera said. Clarkson twitched at this. "Take the pup and go."

"Is there a problem?" asked Boniface.

Nate felt as though his blood itself was boiling, heated by the bright, burning face lingering on the other side of the tracks only a few feet from where he stood. The muscles of his nose tensed to show the fangs protruding from his teeth. He felt his pulse at the roots of the claws pushed through his fingers. His growl broke for breath before continuing.

"Councilor," Shayera said again.

Clarkson approached, uneasy but controlled, as Zarker remained tensed, head down to watch all who surrounded him. Nate saw Clarkson's hand reach out for him.

Nate snapped his jaws. Clarkson pulled away.

"Hold!" Shayera yelled.

Boniface and the others flashed with nervous energy. Dove did not. She remained as bright and overwhelming as ever.

"Come," Clarkson said quietly, putting his hands up for Nate to see. "We go."

"It seems one of your number may have a problem with control," Boniface observed. "The type of problem that could lead to tragedies, like the one you are here to . . . investigate."

Nate remained focused on Dove, growling as Clarkson stretched a hand out for him. She was a fire. Dr. Casey said Riley was lucky to escape the fire after the accident. There was gas but no spark while he was there.

"Against our code," Shayera replied. "Never harm a human."

"So you say."

Nate felt Clarkson's large palm on his shoulder, trying to calm him. He watched as the yellow-orange heads of the others remained trained on him. They were ten in total, surrounding his four. Dove stared as well, her face still burning. Fire would have destroyed any evidence they left behind.

"The Code is precious to us. It is our duty. Like yours."

They must have started it. Dove and Virgil, they needed to cover up their tracks.

"Someone trying to frame us," Shayera said. "Like before."

Dove tilted her head as she watched Nate being pushed away.

"Or perhaps not all of your kind follows your code as strictly as you claim."

"We want peace."

"If this is true, then I suggest you disperse, or assume a less-threatening form."

Zarker growled.

"You have your weapons," Shayera replied, "and we have ours."

"At least we of the Hidden Blade keep our burdens covered."

The metal on Dove's arm appeared as she pushed one sleeve up.

"Tell me, Shadow, have you found anything?"

Shayera was quiet.

"In that case," Boniface continued, "I suggest you allow the facts to determine whether your kind is innocent. And together we may deal with the consequences. Whatever they may be."

Zarker growled once again.

Dove's red hand emerged.

"By our hand," Shayera offered.

"If yours is within reach."

Dove's fingers were twitchy fireflies at the end of her sleeve. Nate felt Clarkson's hand on his shoulder. His former teacher stood between him and the red glow.

"No army keeps peace." Zarker's words were jumbled and broken through his gritted teeth.

"Robert," Shayera whispered, "this isn't the place."

The name struck Nate for a moment. Robert.

137

The Order knew both Shayera and Zarker. Virgil knew him, knew his connection to Riley. Everyone "of the blood" had their birth recorded in the museum archives. The Order must have done something similar. Something more than just following him around.

"We're leaving," continued Shayera, slowly and articulately. "Pax vobiscum," she added with a bow.

"Pax vobiscum," Boniface replied, bowing as well.

"Come," Clarkson exhaled softly, "go now."

Nate felt the light push on his arm. He saw where Shayera and Zarker started to withdraw. Boniface lowered his hands slowly as the others moved back into the trees. Nate turned, allowing Clarkson to usher him away.

Even as he turned his eyes from her, Nate's sense of smell told him that Dove still watched. Her red hand raised. She held the hand out, one finger out and thumb pointed up. She made the motion of a gun firing. "Bang," she said. Then she laughed. She was hot needles in Nate's eyes.

He roared.

Nate tossed Clarkson aside as he swung around. Dove seemed to bounce in his vision, almost dancing. The motion taunted him. She was all he could see—the red right hand, the burning head, the memory of staring down her blade rimmed with his blood. He lunged at her. The tips of his claws scraped the ground. His arm shot up with such force it pulled him onto his toes. The drawstrings on his bag tugged at his shoulders.

Dove slid away. Her scent trail fluttered in front of him. He charged through, the red of her scent mixing with the rage clouding his senses.

There were shouts from all around. Growls and roars followed them in. Nate could see shifts in the colors, the aggression surging through veins, the pops of blades from invisible sleeves. In the swirls of Dove's trailing scent Nate saw the outline of her cloak. It fluttered as she moved, sidestepping and shifting and spinning from his strikes before he could think to make them. He wanted to tear through it. He wanted to embed his claws into her rib cage and tear it open to find her still-beating heart. He wanted the last thing she ever saw to be him plucking it from her chest.

She dodged again. Traces of sweat, heat, adrenaline, and sweet oil followed her. Laughter followed as well, hollow and sharp like the impact of her steps on the ground. It was just as it had been before: she danced circles around him as he swung at emptiness until he could barely stand. He'd had no control then. He paused.

Nate took a moment to watch her movement. The emptiness of her cloak swayed against the cool-hued grays of the dirt and gravel behind her. She was an absence among her surroundings, a blank space in the world—but visible once he knew how to look. She stooped low in front of him, half his height, poised to move in any direction. He then sensed motion elsewhere. The others were moving in to surround him, their blades exposed to the air. Wind whistled past their edges.

Another roar shook Nate's bones. He saw Zarker as a massive red figure, twisting so wildly that those around him shifted away. He shot toward the floating heads coming to surround Nate. Zarker flung long, arcing swipes that pushed the others away. The blackrobes, as he called them. Shayera was a few steps behind, flying like a bullet toward one of the men nearing Nate on the other side. Zarker was a hammer, but Shayera was a scalpel. Nate heard the air push from the man's lungs as she attacked and he launched back. There was no blood on him.

Nate took the chance for another lunge toward Dove. She seemed to shake for a moment. His claws shredded through the tail of her cloak. He growled, eyeing the trail she left behind.

"Learning," she said with a giggle. "Almost."

"Is this your code?" Boniface asked from out of Zarker's reach.

"Get him away!" Shayera yelled from several

feet away. She darted between three of the other blackrobes, holding them near the edge of the trees. Zarker leaped madly between Boniface and five others. Snarls and spit followed his wild twists as he pushed them back. They reeked of panic sweat. They appeared nearly frozen before him, moving forward only when he turned away, and leaping back when he returned. Nate sensed Clarkson rushing up behind him, reaching to grab him once more.

"Is this your innocence?"

"Take him!" Shayera yelled. "Go!"

A flash caught Nate's attention. A sudden impact, dead center in his chest, knocked him back. He staggered from the blow. The pain concentrated in one spot, like he'd been punched by a solid metal tube. The pressure made it hard to breathe. Dove stared up at him as a burning red skull. She was a signal fire in the night. The bluish blade extended behind her, ready to strike. He batted his hands weakly as though trying to swim up for air. The blade flashed toward him. He felt himself falling.

Clarkson wrapped one arm over Nate's shoulders. Dove sprang forward. Clarkson again pulled Nate back. Dove was a red streak, a tracer bullet in the war zone. Clarkson angled in front of him, shielding and pushing Nate away. Dove shot forward once more. There was a wet slice. Dove's blade sprayed blood into the air. Clarkson cried out in pain.

"Get away from here!" Shayera screamed.

Clarkson staggered back. His weight fell toward Nate behind him. Nate sensed the wound, several inches deep, more than halfway through Clarkson's midsection. There was the sharp, rotten scent of acid as his organs bled from inside his body. Nate propped him up by the arms and pulled him away.

"You both go!"

Shayera shot toward another blackrobe on one side of the track. Zarker threw haymakers across three of the others. Dove stood alone in the center of the two rails. She withdrew the cloth from inside of her cloak to wipe the blood from the blade. Shayera and Zarker were red giants holding off spots of color at the edges. Dove was a burning point between them, growing smaller as Nate retreated.

He locked his arm under Clarkson's and pulled until they reached the police barricade at the side of the road. He smelled the blood dripping from under the hand Clarkson clamped over the wound.

"Bad?" Nate asked. It startled him how deep and animal the word sounded in his ears.

Clarkson snarled, pushing away.

"Them?" Nate asked.

"We go," Clarkson replied. He pushed again, not away from Nate, but Nate away from the scene. "They will hold. You must leave."

On the tracks ahead Nate could see where Shayera and Zarker had moved closer to each other. They appeared to move in tandem, holding the blackrobes' attention and keeping them away. He heard Zarker's growl from there. The sound alone could be enough to keep any of the humans from attempting to strike.

"They want you to go," Clarkson said, "you go."

He shoved Nate so hard that it made him step to keep from falling. "Run. I'm behind you," he said with a groan.

Dove had disappeared. Nate took one last look at Shayera and Zarker and those hesitantly surrounding them on each side, Shayera holding them back with feigned swipes and sharp spins while Zarker growled and snapped his jaw. A blackrobe approached Shayera from behind as her attention was drawn away. Zarker shot toward him, thrusting his claw outward.

"Now!" Clarkson screamed as blood hit the air.

Nate sprinted toward the gaps between the trees.

The air carried a scent of fresh moss and moisture, the sound of bubbling and running water. Nate slowed to allow Clarkson to catch up. Clarkson slowed as well. His breaths and steps were heavy with the effort of bounding through the forest, dashing between the trees and hopping around the exposed roots. A steady drip of blood trailed him.

Nate came to a stop at the bank of a narrow stream. Cool blue-green water lapped at the bank, rippling off rocks and roots damp with moss. Tree tops swayed gently, branches creaking and groaning. There was no camel-shaped rock, that was on the other side of the preserve. An owl hovered in the distance as a few small animals, maybe weasels or more shrews like he had sensed before, slept inside their burrow.

Clarkson yanked at the bag strap stretched across his chest. He let the laptop bag drop into the dirt. His arm didn't move from the puncture in his abdomen. It still bled under his hand. His tongue hung from the side of his mouth. He exhaled spit as he staggered up to the water, knelt, and crawled to the edge of the stream.

"Stop," Nate said as Clarkson inched his snout toward the water. "Unclean."

"For humans," Clarkson replied before lapping at the running stream.

Nate sniffed the wind: trees, grass, dirt, moss, water, the other animals in their holes or in the trees, Clarkson and his blood and spit, and the very minor sting of chemicals in the water. He tried to focus on the forest where they had come from. Their trail went too far for him to track.

"Okay?" Nate asked as Clarkson twisted to sit on the bank.

"Can heal now," he replied. "Hard to heal when running."

Nate tried to get the words out but all he could manage was, "Them?"

Clarkson took a long breath. He shook his head. "Very strong, but . . . " He huffed. "We cannot help them." He reached back to dip one large mitt into the stream. Water dripped between his fingers as he placed the hand against the wound. He groaned, rubbing the water through the hair over his skin.

"Dove," Nate said.

"Yes. We know her," Clarkson said as he reached for another handful.

Nate let out a short growl.

Clarkson wiped the blood from around the hole. "If Dove wanted to kill, I would be dead." He watched as Nate stepped toward the water. "Warning tonight. Not killing."

Nate saw the traces of chemicals as putrid green dots, miniscule within the cleaner colors of the water. It didn't seem too bad. He remembered his mother yelling at him not to drink the water at Patrick Wallace Creek. Why would she tell him that if it only affected humans? He reached one hand in to scoop some water out. It tasted like nothing. It was the first time he'd drank or eaten anything while changed. He shook the water from his hand and laid down to lap his tongue in the stream. It felt nice in his mouth and throat. He closed his eyes and took a deep breath. It felt as though the coolness filled his senses, washing away the residual heat left from the encounter only minutes before. He'd forgotten to do that before, imagine his breath cooling him, as Ulrich had instructed.

"Nice," Clarkson whispered. "Some things feel better like this."

Nate slid away from the creek side. He knelt next to where Clarkson kept one hand over the hole in his midsection. Its odor had lessened. Clarkson lifted his palm to check the wound. "Getting older," Clarkson said, covering the wound again. "Healing takes longer."

"I . . . " Nate started but couldn't continue as he wanted. "There," he pointed in the direction of their tracks. "I . . . I," he struggled to get his tongue and stiff lips to form the words as he wanted, "sh . . . should not . . . not be there."

"You had to be. We went for you."

Nate titled his head at this.

"Council wants to see how you act with us."

Nate snarled. Shayera and Boniface had the situation under control. Then Dove appeared. But it was

Nate who provoked the attack as the two sides were parting. "Not good," he said again.

"Understand," Clarkson replied, wincing as he pushed himself to sit higher. "Dove is . . ." He took a long breath. " . . . dangerous. You have reason to fear her."

"Not fear," Nate snapped.

"Should be. She is their strongest. She is . . ." Clarkson shook his head as he trailed off.

"What?" Nate insisted.

Clarkson shook his head once more before turning back to the stream.

Nate dropped down next to a root which arched into and under the water. He sat how it was comfortable: back straight and neck bent forward, legs bent with knees up and off the ground, both hands placed in front of him. His bag settled nicely between his shoulder blades. It reminded him of the way a dog sits. It *was* the way a dog sits.

He lifted his head to what he could see between the leaves hanging off the trees. The sky was a big, gray blank overhead. No stars or clouds in front of them, just nothing. Nothing up there to smell from down here. It was empty space with scents wafting far in front of it, as though nothing existed beyond what was immediately around him. There was comfort in the thought, like the world was smaller and he was more important in it. But he still missed the stars.

Clarkson had dulled to an easy yellow color. He stretched side to side as he remained seated upright at the edge of the bank. He was smaller than the others, smaller than Nate even, and not as powerfully built. He didn't have Zarker's wild spiked mane nor Shayera's sleek outline. He was rounder, more refined, as though his hair had been trimmer on the forearms and shoulders. Nate couldn't help wondering if Clarkson had ever been in a fight before. If he hadn't, why was he assigned to come with them when Ulrich had to know there was the possibility of the Order coming? He figured it was to have someone Nate knew and would be comfortable having along, but it seemed too arrogant to think Ulrich would send someone else just for him. Still, Shayera called him the leader.

"Why go for me?" Nate asked, the words coming easier but still limited.

"Your father and mother were both High Councilors."

"My mother?"

"Yes. After your father. Before Ulrich. You are unique among us." Clarkson nodded. "We expect much."

Nate snorted. "Feels . . . not that way."

"Council pushes. Council tests. But Council is loyal. We all are."

Clarkson pressed his shoulders back and his chest out, pushing the little paunch at his belly. He groaned with each movement. It made sense that a person's human form would influence their altered one. That would be why Shayera was long and lean, and why Zarker was messy and savage.

Nate wondered what his dad had looked like.

Was the beard part of his appearance as well, the way Zarker's long facial hair was a tuft of hair at his chin and throat? People told Nate that he was taller than his father but that otherwise he looked the same. If they looked alike as people would they look alike as wolves?

And what about his mother? Would he ever see her in this form? Had anyone seen her this way since she apparently left the Council? Perhaps she was right to withdraw from them, retreat into a quiet, isolated life with her son, never even telling him about what he was. When she told him not to drink the creek water was it because she didn't know it only affected humans, that she thought it would affect him while in human form, or because she really didn't want him to know? Would his father have told him sooner?

Nate felt another pang of guilt for the way their conversation had ended that night. He didn't even believe what Maier said, but some part of him still wanted her to hear it. He'd apologize in the morning. If he ever managed to return.

Nate stretched for the creek for another drink. He noticed a vague grayish shape as he lowered toward the water. He leaned closer. The shape did the same. He turned slightly. Sharp angles traced the outline in front of him, gray and blurry along the water's surface and among the haze of scent. The silhouette resembled that of a dog drawn crude and savage, with jagged lines in the place of rounder, softer ones. He stared and huffed at the figure in the water. The figure did the same to him. He watched his head shake back at him. Strands of fur grew out from his cheeks, up to a pair of outwardly pointed ears, with more fur, short and spiked, lining the top of his head. His eyes were faded gray shadows on the rippling creek, not the red he'd seen in others. This wasn't him. Not the person he'd known for his entire life. Not even the person others saw now, whether through scent or through sight. This was someone else. Something else. Perhaps it would be best if he never saw himself or even his mother like this again. He didn't have to worry about seeing his father this way. He swiped one hand through the water until the reflection disappeared behind the cold blue.

Clarkson exhaled a long, calming breath.

"Better?" Nate asked as he pulled away from the creek side.

"Getting there," croaked Clarkson.

"Museum?" Nate asked. It wasn't an easy word to stretch his lips around.

Clarkson shook his head before going back for more water.

"Safe house," Clarkson said after gulping down what spilled from his hand. "Friend at the edge of the woods."

"Where?"

"No," Clarkson said, wiping his mouth as Nate had. "You go home. Go to your mom."

"Why?"

Clarkson growled as he rose from the water. "Because she would want that."

Nate offered his hand to help Clarkson steady himself on his feet but was waved off as Clarkson secured the tight strap across his chest, the bag pressing snugly against him. He gestured for Nate to go. Nate took a moment to key in on the smells of the town, the old grease and garbage, exhaust, sweat, and smoke. From there he could find his way home, following on the outside from within the trees. He ran once again, sensing Clarkson in the distance until he wasn't there anymore.

Birds began to flutter. Morning was coming soon. Nate sprinted toward the outside of the town. Home. Where no one would see him this way. Ever.

CHAPTER 8

It was past noon before Nate finally wandered down the stairs, hearing the murmur of the television grow closer with every step. He couldn't remember the last time he'd slept in that late, but considering the time he'd gotten home, and everything that had happened the day before—the tense meeting with Riley, the equally tense one with Ulrich and Maier, and finally the increasingly tense encounter at the tracks and subsequent flight through the woods—he needed the rest. He didn't dream. In fact, he hadn't dreamed at all over the two months since that night . . . the first change, the incident, the end of an equally ridiculous day. He'd slept late that morning as well, not by choice.

Although, if he was honest with himself, a big part of his reluctance to wake up was the quietly tense conversation he'd had with his mother. Between the day, night, and morning he'd had, he could hardly remember their conversation. He did clearly remember her stomping off to bed. Finally, after hours of sporadic sleep, he figured he couldn't avoid her any longer. That was another detriment of not having a door on either his room or his "apartment": it was difficult to hide.

The daytime talk show came into view as he descended the stairs into the living room. Indents remained on the armrest on her side of the couch. Her bedroom door was open. She wasn't there. Farther down he saw the light across the floor in front of the study under the stairs. He concentrated, trying to ignore the sound of some guy on the television telling the women in the audience how they could be more attractive and therefore successful, and heard the tapping of computer keys and the weak click of a mouse. He closed his eyes, took a deep breath, and continued down the stairs.

"So, ummm . . . " he started as he turned toward the open door of the study. His mother sat at the rolltop desk. "I—"

"Where did you go last night?" she asked without turning away from the computer.

"Nowhere," he said out of instinct.

He could see her disappointment in the way her shoulders dropped. He immediately regretted telling her that. His mind raced back to the starless sky above the stream where Clarkson sat to recover. He had decided there that he would apologize to her. His lips moved but the words didn't come. No explanation came to mind, no excuse for even lying just now, not even the simplest words possible: I'm sorry. There was just . . . nothing.

"You know I never wanted this for you," she said again without turning.

He squeezed his eyes shut. It felt like the last late

morning he'd had, waking up in the hospital. The words were there but he couldn't bring them out.

"That's why I never told you." She turned but not far enough to see him. "I always planned to. Thirteenth birthday. Fourteenth. Fifteenth. It just . . . " She went back to the computer, slouching in the old chair. "It was never right."

"I don't blame you," he finally said.

Her face came into view just over her shoulder. Red lines rolled down from her eyes.

"But you don't trust me," she said.

He looked away.

He looked at the old map on the wall with Transylvania. If the place actually existed, then did its fabled vampires exist as well? He already knew of one B-horror monster that was real. He looked at the photo albums at the bottom of the bookshelf. It had been a few years since he looked, but he couldn't imagine there being any photos of either his mother or father in their altered forms. He looked at the cracked spines of history books.

Would they include mention of Fenrei and black-robes, or even Transylvania? He looked at the yellowing newspapers with headlines of murders in the town. Almost twenty years the town had gone without an unexplained murder, but that had ended two nights ago.

"I went with some of the others to check out the murder scene. We needed to know if there was anything we could find while we were . . . changed."

She turned in the chair. The tear lines were clear down her face. "Who did you go with?"

"Mr. Clarkson, a lady named Shayera, and a big guy named Zarker. I saw them once before—"

"Zarker?" she said, eyes widening with surprise.

"Yeah. Real name is Robert I think."

"What happened?" She turned in the chair to face him. She looked as though she'd cried longer than she'd slept. "And don't say 'nothing.'"

"We were checking out the scene when a group of blackrobes came from the trees."

His mother twitched at the word "blackrobes."

"Everything seemed fine until," he closed his eyes with a sigh. He shook his head knowing what he had to say next. "I saw Dove there. I was told to leave but she, Dove, she just . . . " Nate's eyes squeezed shut. He turned to the ground before opening them again so that he wouldn't have to look at her. "She provoked me into going after her. After that . . . I dunno . . . Clarkson pulled me away. He got hurt but we ran, and he healed, and that was it." He returned his attention to his mother. Her brow was lined with concern.

"Is that *all* that happened?"

"I don't know," he said, uncomfortably. "I don't know what happened with Shayera and Zarker. I smelled blood as I was leaving. I think Zarker might've . . . "

She exhaled a long breath, turning the side of her face to him.

"Might've what?"

"Attacked one of them. The . . . people."

"Damn," his mother muttered, shaking her head.

Her eyes closed in thought. "Did you find anything before that?"

"No. Some of Dawn's blood on the tracks."

His mother shook her head again, eyes still closed.

"I'm not even sure why we went there."

"It was to get you involved with the Council," she said, turning back to the computer. "To get you some experience."

"Mr. Clarkson said something like that."

"High Councilors do that for those with . . . promise," his mother muttered.

"Is something wrong?" he finally asked.

She drew a breath before sliding the chair closer to the bookshelf.

She clicked from the email she had been writing to another open browser tab. The *Stumpvale Daily* website blared the headline "Murder Mystery Continues as Family Found Dead."

Nate ran his eyes over the story on-screen: an entire family in their house near the edge of the forest, found in one room stacked on top of each other.

"Liam Bailey," his mother said as he continued down the article, "the girl's boyfriend."

Signs of struggle, claw marks, blood everywhere.

"Him, his parents, his little brother. All of them."

Something about thick white hairs.

"I—" Nate stuttered, staring at the short paragraphs on-screen, "I didn't know. I mean, I didn't know him well. Do you think any of them could have been the one that Zarker—"

"No," his mother said. She clicked back to her email account. She scrolled up the line of messages faster than he could read. "I've been talking to friends at the police department and the paper. They're doing their best to limit the information until we can figure out what's going on. This was done inside the house. The murders and . . . "

Nate felt his mouth hanging slightly open in shock.

" . . . this."

She clicked on a file attached to one of the messages. An image opened of a light brown wall with the camera flash reflecting off. Blood dripped from letters scribbled across the wall, as though taken from a Hannibal Lecter movie. "GOD'S GIFT"

Nate glanced from the computer to his mother. Her lip trembled. The slight lines in her face turned down.

"What does that mean?" he asked.

She took another long breath.

"It's your name."

CHAPTER 9

"I'm sorry but Diane isn't in the office this morning, Ms. McKnight."

"Do you know why?" Riley said over her phone to Brenda at Green and Rivera.

"She said it was a family emergency."

"Family emergency?" Riley wondered aloud. "Is there another way I can contact her?"

"I'm sorry, Ms. McKnight, but we're not allowed to give out other people's personal information. If you would like to schedu—"

"No," Riley snapped. "Sorry, I mean, not right now, thanks."

"Is there anything else I can help you with, Ms. McKnight?" Brenda asked, impatience growing in her tone.

"No," Riley said. Family emergency repeated in her mind.

"Very good. Have a nice d—"

Riley ended the call.

Family emergency. Diane, Riley's physical therapist at Green and Rivera. Sister Kennera, Riley's contact with the Order. *Family* emergency.

"Hey Mom!" Riley yelled from her room. She rolled around on the bed to reach for the cast. The motion caused little jolts of pain throughout the leg, a reminder that she was still healing. "Mom!" she yelled again. She slapped the plastic cast over her thigh, yanking the straps so tight that she felt the blood moving through her leg.

"Yes?" she barely heard her mom from outside. There were rushed footsteps on the floor. Riley snapped the knee piece into place and reached for the boot. There was one quick knock on the door before the knob turned. "I'm here," her mom said as she opened the door, "are you—"

"I need to borrow the car," Riley said, looking down as she threaded the boot straps through the plastic slits.

"Oh . . . " Her mom said. "Where do you need to go? Maybe I can—"

"I'd rather take myself." Riley pulled the last strap into place. "You know, just. . ." Riley started. She looked up at her mother standing in the frame of her bedroom door. Her mother had one arm across her stomach, fingers timidly rubbing at the opposite elbow. Riley felt the pity coming through on her face. "I want to do this for myself," she said softly, "so I'll know I can."

Her mother took a moment to form a sheepish smile. "That's fine," she said, adding a nod. "I'll leave the keys next to the door for you."

"Thanks, Mom."

"Take your time, hon." Riley's mom turned

to step out. She stopped. "You want this open or closed?"

"Open's fine. Thanks."

"No problem, dear."

If they didn't want her knowing how to get to their meeting place, they would have blindfolded her, like they do in the spy movies. Or driven her around and taken a different route every time. Of course in a town as small as theirs, with only about a dozen main roads connecting everywhere to everywhere else, it would be hard to get thoroughly lost, even with the blindfold. There could be thirty minutes of driving in loops, but as soon as the blindfold comes off, oh hey, it's the Cunningham's old place. The people could be anonymous, there were enough of them for that, always coming and going, but locations never were. Only the memories changed.

Riley stopped on the street before the dirt road

toward the barn in the woods. She peeked through the gap between the old buildings that stood on the border between town and forest. The chain across the dirt road was lowered. Either someone had left the path open, or not everyone had a key. She backed up and took the turn onto the dirt road.

Her mom's old Honda shook with every bump and dip, not like Diane's sleek sedan. Riley felt the vibrations through the seat and into her leg. She flinched as her front right tire hit a hole. She flinched again when the rear tire did the same. Her crutches slid across the front edge of the passenger seat and clanked loudly against the window. One fell into the gap between the seat and the door. She swore, then groaned as the car bounced off another bump in the road. It was her first time driving since before that night.

Several cars lined the flatter side of the path. The chain remained stretched across the road. Riley stopped and backed up to the end of the cars hastily parked along the side of a dirt road leading toward a chained-off path in front of a metal barn so rusted it looked like it would collapse if a bird landed on it. "Yeah," she muttered as she too pulled off the road, "that doesn't look at all suspicious." Her leg shook as the driver's side of her car hung over a slope at the end of the road. She gritted her teeth.

She grabbed at her crutches. She tugged at the one that had fallen, seeing where it wedged perfectly against the door's armrest at the end of the footwell. She leaned onto her good leg, stretched one arm out, and pulled at the metal pole. The yanking caused shocking tremors to run through the still-broken bone. She roared, pounding the seat next to her. Should have been so easy to simply slide over, reach across the seat, and lift the crutch from inside the gap. Or even easier, just park the car, get out, and walk. But here she was, struggling to accomplish the simplest thing, and pain was shooting through half of her body. It was pathetic. Pathetic and broken. She gritted her teeth and gave one hard pull before the crutch popped out of place.

It didn't feel right coming out here alone. It didn't even feel right coming out here with Diane. At least not without telling someone. Her mom she kept secrets from. She barely told her much about Remy. Nate was the one who'd normally listen, including during times when she suspected he wasn't interested or didn't want to know. It was hard not telling him about everything she was going through: the frustration of barely being able to walk twenty steps without aching, that sitting caused pain, how annoying it was to carry crutches to the bathroom, how every little shake and rattle during a car ride made her entire side throb. About how she'd learned that werewolves—monsters—lived alongside them. He already blamed himself for not being able to protect her from an accident he couldn't have stopped. He'd drive himself crazy thinking she'd be hurt again from something he couldn't possibly control. Of all the experiences they'd shared together, this was one she had to keep to herself.

Virgil had said it was the purpose of the Order

to protect the innocent from ever knowing such a threat exists. Better he not know. Nate, her mom, Remy's family, Janey, Beth, Shaunna, the rest of the team, everyone at school, anyone not already involved. There was enough suspicion over what happened to Dawn. Anything else would cause a panic. Better he never know.

She took a deep breath before finally opening the door for the long walk along unsteady ground before the even longer, more perilous journey down the stairs. She could already hear the rhythm of her two hard crutches and one soft step on the stone floors. Heavy-soft. Heavy-soft.

"Where are you?"

"Beneath the shroud."

"Where do you wish to be?"

"Bathed in the light."

Riley peeked in as the door slid open. One man

was visible in the gap. He wore the long-sleeved cloak that she'd seen during sparring. The hood covered his head and an extra piece of fabric covered most of his face, leaving everything else, she assumed just his eyes, in complete shadow. He kept his hands down and folded in front of him, his sleeves covering his fingers. He remained still as the door opened, then stepped back to allow her through.

Two other men were in the room with him, one of them tall, possibly the same one she'd seen last time. He motioned for her to pass. The metal cuff was visible on the back of his hand, without the glove to cover it. One long rifle was propped against the wall next to the stairs. The last of the three men was short and stocky, possibly the other recruit she'd seen thoroughly embarrassed by Dove. She couldn't be sure through the coverings which rendered them faceless. They were shadows made solid. She nodded as she crutched by.

The sound of metal scrapes and clanks grew louder as she cautiously lowered from one stair to the next. Then there was a quick pause in the noise before, "Again!" And the scrapes, clanks, and grunts began anew.

She positioned her foot at the end of each stair before taking the short hop down to the next. Wouldn't take much for her to slip; leaning too far forward or back, some mud or water tracked in from outside. The result would be unstoppable, a painful plunge down the thirty or so steps it took to reach the bottom of the staircase. At that point she'd either be broken, even more than she already was, or dead.

The air in the tunnel was thick with humidity. Riley felt as though she could the taste the sweat as she reached the last few stairs, gritting her teeth against the constant vibration in her leg. The noise was enough to drown out the sound of her hollow poles hitting the stone floor. "Again!" Shadows danced through the opening into the main chamber, so many that she couldn't count the sources. The first door over the glass case was left slightly open. Only six swords remained from the long row it typically housed. The case of daggers was the same: nearly empty. A couple of revolvers had been removed as well as two of the long rifles. The blunderbusses sat untouched. The sounds of struggle ahead easily drowned out her own.

"Again!"

She glanced at the second-to-last portrait on the wall. Her father's stoic expression looked back. The helmet of black hair, the solid chin with the deep scar cutting through it, the uniform; he was more a soldier than a father. Was the blade on his arm as he sat for that picture? He had been in the army before she was born, even before he met her mother, but this wasn't the army she knew from the faded, green jacket with the "McKnight" patch stitched over the front pocket. This was a different army. A forgotten army with its own mission and methods. Its own rules.

"Again!" shouted the voice from inside the central chamber. Shadows danced in time to the music of metal sliding off metal and grunts before every thrust.

Riley could hardly see the opening at the other side of the room through the bodies gathered inside. They stood in lines of sparring pairs. Long swords flashed through the thin light overhead, feet shuffled forward and back, men and a few women clenched their jaws as they attacked and dodged. They stopped, freezing in place, one thrusting a sword while the other turned it away. It seemed odd that they'd train with swords in-hand when their weapons were on their wrists.

The pairs fell back to a starting position. They faced each other, swords up in parallel lines, tapering from her like a row of crops or trees stretching into the sky. "Again!" shouted the voice which she still couldn't pinpoint as it seemed to come from every surface in the round, domed room. Every pair moved in coordination: one strike, one block, one thrust, one parry, and repeat the other way before, "Again!" The movements repeated. "Again!" The people didn't even appear to think. Riley leaned to see through the rows as they reset, finally bringing Virgil into view on the other side of the room. She locked her eyes on him until he looked toward her, then she flinched away.

The movement stopped. There was no call of "Again!" Instead, there were tapped footsteps on the floor as Virgil approached.

"What are you doing here?" came the voice of broken rocks.

Riley didn't respond. She stared at the wall of still shadows. The lines of people cast a series of overlapping heads and shoulders. "Again!" The shadows danced.

"I don't have time for another broken thing," Virgil said, turning to walk away.

"What happened?" Riley asked.

"The corruption happened," Virgil replied, looking back only enough to see her at the very edge of his sight. "The Canaanites have violated the peace we've worked for centuries to protect. They have attacked the innocent."

Riley furrowed her brow at this.

"Hours after one of our brothers was slain while investigating Dawn Musgrave's crime site, others were found. Other bodies. The boy. His family."

Riley looked down to the floor. The dim shadows crisscrossed each other from every angle, lightening and darkening in motion. She felt as though she should've been sadder about this news. Another fellow student, someone she could have known better. Instead, her view dropped farther, the hollow poles at her sides, the hard plastic boot with the Velcro that she felt digging into her skin, and the one good leg which she could still stand on. The motion continued to cast its shadow over her. It was an easy back and forth. Repetition made it automatic.

"You are not one of us," Virgil said. "Leave."

He took one step away.

"My father was," she said.

"Yes. He was."

"Father Pius the Third," Riley added. "Your leader."

Virgil looked back again. "I wasn't here for much of his stewardship, but I considered him a friend."

"You said he was the best you'd ever seen."

"He was." Virgil faced her, lifting his chin to stare down at her through the bottom of his eyes. "Not all are born into this life. Many are unfit. But I have never seen one more suited to our mission than Father Pius. And, I had hoped, you."

Riley looked again at the floor, an innocent, she thought. "Again!" she heard in the room. "Again!" she heard in her mind.

She'd take her position in the corner of the spring mat, her feet an inch away from the white trim on either side. It was two steps into a double handspring into a frontflip into another double handspring and second frontflip with a twist into the opposite corner. Stopping off the second flip was the problem. If she could control her momentum through the motion, the rest was automatic. The tumbles and cartwheels, the pirouette for artistry and the shoulder brush for attitude, even the double-back-handspring-backflip-tumble-handstand to frontflip-backspring-backflip with a twist sequence at the end came to her immediately. It helped not to think.

The layers of shadow shifted on the floor. Virgil waited for them to stop before stepping away.

"They don't move like Dove does," Riley said.

Virgil paused. He turned toward her, flanked by two rows of people pointing long swords in the air.

"Not all are born into this life," he repeated. "These are recruits, not warriors. Fate will soon decide whether they follow this path or find another."

"And what about me?" Riley asked, crutching one step closer to him. "Am I a recruit?"

"You're a failed experiment," he said gravely. "You're unfulfilled potential."

She scowled at him.

He leaned back, pointing his chin at her. The others in the room didn't move but she could see them straining to keep their blades pointed up and their backs from slouching.

"You can fix me," she said.

"No," Virgil replied. "You can."

"How?"

"Commitment. Faith. Absolute devotion to a cause greater than yourself." He moved toward her. Riley saw those swords raised around him lower slightly as he stepped away. "Your father understood these things. He absorbed them, made them a part of his being. Perhaps some part of him exists through you. A part that will make you greater than you could have ever been."

Her gaze sank to the floor again.

"But," he added, "perhaps we will never know."

"Again!" The scrapes and grunts resumed.

Her head remained lowered. The floor routine repeated in her mind with its flips and spins and sudden shifts of momentum. She felt the ache in her leg, then in her hands and arms from holding her up. She struggled even to pull a crutch from a car seat.

"The doctors said it could be a year before I'm healed."

"If you are willing to commit yourself to our cause—your father's cause—your healing will be complete. Now and forever."

The lights overhead dimmed all but the edges of his face. The jagged lines at his cheeks, eyes and forehead were cracks in the concrete. "How?" she asked.

"You will know when the time comes, but not before then."

"If I become a recruit."

"No, if you become a pilgrim."

The gathered mass shuffled its feet.

"One of us."

It groaned and breathed as one.

"Our sister."

"Again!" shouted the voice bouncing off every

wall. There was an audible sigh just before the first move.

"Then you will be a part of our cause. You will heal. You will know."

"Know what?"

"The truth about your father and yourself. Where you came from and what you were born for. You will know your true potential and, Lord willing, you will live it. You will never again be a broken little girl."

"Again!"

"This is a big decision, Riley. Our requirements are difficult. Not all who wish to join are able."

Riley stared up at him. His eyes were dark. Shadows ran through the lines tracing toward light-rimmed ends. His face was a reverse of the sun.

"But you," he said, giving a solemn nod toward her, "you were born for this."

The figures danced behind him. Their shadows stretched across the floor. She imagined the eyes of the portrait behind her. Her father's eyes would forever watch her here. Different than she remembered but there he was. And he would always be.

"Where are you, Riley?" Virgil asked.

"Beneath the shroud."

"Where do you wish to be?"

"Bathed in the light."

CHAPTER 10

THE SIGN OUT FRONT SAID THE MUSEUM WAS closed for a private event. A single guard redirected annoyed parents, disappointed children, and relieved teenagers toward the parking lot. Nate waited until the last set of visitors had started down the stairs before approaching. He locked eyes with the guard, a man he couldn't remember ever seeing before. "Mr. Wallace," the guard said with a nod. Nate gave the door a good push to enter.

The front area was completely empty, not even a woman behind the desk. The main gallery was empty as well. Walking under the blue whale skeleton without the sound of visitors talking among each other gave the scene an eerie feeling. It was the kind of scenario where characters whisper, "It's quiet," followed by, "Too quiet," before a monster attacks. Or, perhaps, the "monsters" are attacked. He still looked up as he passed under the skeleton. It was his habit.

He continued into the second gallery. The emptiness made it appear bigger than usual. Evidence of life, both natural and manmade, filled the room, but there was no life itself. There were only remnants of what had once existed. The scraps and leftovers. The remains. The Baileys. They once existed and now were nothing but remains. He pushed the back of his keycard to the pad next to the door at the rear of the gallery. There was life inside.

Harsh grunts and snaps raged down the hallway. The crowd spilled out from the main room and into the hall. The other voices quieted enough for one to be heard.

"—obvious move against us," it said. Nate

cautiously approached before remembering that some in the room would smell him as soon as the front door opened, if not sooner. "We can't allow their aggression to go unchallenged." There were nods and growls of approval.

Members of the crowd turned as he neared. The whispers grew as the crowd became more aware of him. They parted to lead him toward the middle of the main chamber.

"It's him."

"Is his mother here?"

"—nothing like his dad."

"—started it all—"

"—about time someone did something—"

"—his fault—"

Nate saw Maier looking at him from over his shoulder, as though Nate had interrupted him during some grand oration. Zarker was again at his side. The other side of the room had Ulrich with Shayera a step behind him, on the opposite side of where he had stood the day before. Nate was happy for a moment to see Shayera there unharmed. The lower portion of the tapestry was invisible behind the crowd packed against the walls, leaving a small circle in the middle where Maier was standing, and a wide gap between Zarker and everyone else. He stood a head taller and nearly twice as wide as all the others.

"Another witness," Maier said, gesturing toward Nate as he stepped through the path into the center of the room. "We may argue about who is at fault for recent events, but blame is not the question any longer," Maier continued. "The real question before this council is how many more atrocities must we endure before action is taken?" There were more growls and shouts of approval.

Ulrich waited for the murmurs to settle before speaking. "While I agree these latest murders are horrific, I don't agree that we should allow them to cloud our judgment. This isn't the first time some rogue actor has attempted to provoke our kind into endangering ourselves. Remember the night hunts in New Amsterdam, Dresden, and London?" There were nods and grunts at this as well. "Remember the attack on our own High Councilor?" Nate shot a questioning look as Ulrich continued. "Unsanctioned actions that were met with swift justice. We were wise in our refusal to respond then, though members of this council suggested otherwise." Ulrich looked at everyone except Maier as he spoke, making it clear whom he was speaking of.

Maier stood with his hands clasped behind his back. His torso ran almost straight down to his waist, which was almost straight through his legs and to the floor. His frame was a solid block.

Nate took a moment to look over the rest of the room. Even those men and women who'd nodded when Maier spoke—with their scowls and arms folded at Ulrich—still looked at the High Councilor with respect. They were in opposition, but they weren't enemies. He wondered if it was that way within the Order as well.

"The difference here is that the blackrobes have

made a play for attention." Maier looked to Nate as he said this. Nate couldn't tell if he were doing so because of what was written on the wall at the crime scene or simply as part of his delivery. He looked over others as well. "They have not only set us up for a crime, twice, but they have demonstrated a willingness to expose us and our gifts, an act strictly forbidden by our Accord."

"So you would have us reveal ourselves, then?" Ulrich countered. "Allow a moment of fear to undo centuries of careful work?"

Maier glanced over to Nate again. "This pup," Maier said with one hand pointed at Nate, "foolish and rash as his actions may have been, is not incorrect. We have seen the Order's intent. They prepare for war while we prepare for debate."

"Allowing one young man's temper to prompt us to act would only prove ourselves the monsters they so fear."

Zarker growled, "Should be afraid."

Maier raised one hand to silence him.

"While I respect your intentions, High Councilor, even you must admit that the time of secrecy has passed. What was possible for our ancestors isn't possible in this new world of unlimited information. Sooner or later our existence will be revealed. Better we do it ourselves than have it done for us." More agreement from the crowd.

Ulrich seemed to roll his eyes. "Yesterday you were ready to punish 'the pup' for possibly exposing our secret, and today you are advocating for that very action."

Maier didn't hesitate. "Last night's events changed my mind."

Neither did Ulrich. "And that's precisely why this council exists. To keep our kind safe from the mood swings of a dictator. We don't make decisions for today, we make decisions for generations."

"At least I am able to make a decision." There was a noticeable gasp in the room. "At least I'm willing to do what it takes to protect our kind instead of allowing outsiders to threaten us," Maier continued.

The loose skin hanging from Ulrich's chin tightened as he jutted his jaw. Annoyance grew in the old man's face.

"It isn't the Order." Nate immediately regretted speaking, again. He could see Clarkson in the crowd beyond Shayera. The old lady from the ticket booth was in there as well as Mrs. Wald, and others who looked familiar but he didn't know. He looked to the floor and went silent, feeling their stares.

"Who is it, then?" Maier asked.

Nate lifted his eyes to meet Maier's stare. He had dipped his foot in the water. Nothing left but to jump in. "Shayera was negotiating with them." He glanced to where Shayera stood alongside Ulrich. "We were leaving, until the woman—"

"Which woman?" Maier asked.

"Dove," Nate said as though the name were poison in his mouth.

"Sister Dove," Maier said, throwing his hands out and looking around. "Father Vigilius's first lieutenant." He then focused on Ulrich. "Do you honestly believe that Sister Dove would act without a direct order from Vigilius himself?"

"The Prior is no fool," Ulrich countered. "He knows that an all-out conflict would harm his kind as much as it would ours. Perhaps even more, as it would cut them off from the source of their power."

Nate furrowed his brow at this. *Source of their power?*

"Yet they seem to welcome it," Maier said.

"Then let them be the monsters," replied Ulrich.

"Inevitable," Zarker growled loudly.

"Nothing is inevitable." Ulrich answered with sagely calm. Most of the crowd nodded. "It's serendipitous that Patrick Wallace's son is here as we have this discussion," Ulrich continued. Nate again felt their eyes on him, but this time their looks were accusatory rather than curious. "When I first assumed this post I promised my predecessors that I would do everything within my power to keep this community safe, exactly as his parents did." More agreement in the crowd. "High Councilor Wallace and Father Pius didn't always agree, but in the end they were able to work for our mutual interests. Father Vigilius is still new in his post. We should allow him the opportunity to put his house in order before we accuse him of high crimes against the Accord."

Nate shook his head. "No." Eyes returned to him. "Virgil is the problem. He and Dove, they provoked me two months ago, before I even knew what I was. They provoked me into action last night." He glanced to Shayera. She stared through him. "And they have provoked me now, with this new murder."

Ulrich started. "How have they—"

"My name is on the wall!"

Ulrich tilted his head in intrigue.

"Nathaniel, from the Hebrew meaning 'God has given,'" Nate recited from the pair of baby naming sites his mother had shown him. "They wrote my name at a murder scene."

He could feel the skepticism of those surrounding him.

"I don't know why they're doing this," he said, "but Virgil, Vigilius, Highlander, whatever he's called—he can't be trusted."

"The pup is right," Maier said.

"The *pup* doesn't speak for this council," Ulrich replied, "and neither do you."

"My father did," said Nate.

"You aren't your father."

"My mother as well," Nate added. "The same parents who gave me this . . . " He raised his hands from his sides. " . . . gift." He looked at them. Their soft human flesh was far from the rough, scaled skin he and everyone else in the room could change into. "If this is my inheritance, then give me all of it." He could see confusion scattered across many of the faces in the room. "There was a reason you sent me out last night. Let me serve."

Gasps and whispers cluttered the air. Some were angry.

"Why not?" Maier said with a laugh. "If the pup

fancies himself fit to lead, let him try." He surveyed the room. "I call for a vote of appointment."

Zarker snarled.

"Enough," Ulrich said, still so calm. "Perhaps one day Mr. Wallace will be qualified to assume a place of leadership in our community but for now he is still too unknown in our ways. As fortuitous as it was to have him here, his presence has become a distraction." Ulrich glanced over his left shoulder before gesturing toward Nate.

Shayera immediately stepped forward, her tank top displaying the toned muscles that stretched down her arms.

He exhaled loudly to speak, but her look silenced him, as though she could rip Nate's head off if she wanted. Lingering stares followed as he moved from the center of the chamber and into the hall. Ulrich resumed speaking once he was out of sight.

Nate saw Shayera's lean arm over his shoulder. "What happened last night?" he whispered.

No answer. She continued walking.

He stopped at the door. He turned to face her. His eyes were level with the top of her head. He pushed back his shoulders as if to intimidate her. "What happened?" he said again.

She took one step to the side, leaned, reached out, and pushed the door open behind him. "Out," she said.

He stepped back just as the door came swinging inward. He put his arm back to stop the door from hitting him. "Did you kill them?"

"Out," she repeated.

He stepped back into the gallery outside. "What happened?"

"We of the blood shall never harm a human," she said as the door closed. "Remember that."

The slamming door echoed throughout the room. The noise spread outward. Then all that remained was silence. Silence, still, empty, and dead.

CHAPTER 11

"WE WERE BORN INTO A BEAUTIFUL WORLD. All of us. A world free from corruption and evil."

Virgil turned down the hall behind the main chamber.

Riley took a last look at the recruits swinging wooden training swords at each other. They were clumsy and awkward, swinging too hard and too wide, nearly tripping over themselves. There was no grace in their movements. Not like there was with Dove. Not like there had been with her.

Virgil waited expectantly. "But you are not here

for dogma," he said, stepping into motion down the hall which carried farther under the ground behind the rusted barn. She followed, hearing the sound of her crutches bounce off every surface. A few candles, hung from metal holders at the highest points of the arches, splashed flickering yellow light upon the floor. Darkness spread between them. She thought of the night she saw Virgil as she sat with Nate in front of her apartment. The streetlight shined through the strands of hair pulled over his head. The candles did the same thing now, reflecting off his high-collared white shirt and making his head glow and fade. They had called him Highlander then, joked that he was an alien invader. They'd watched movies, talking about nothing. Maybe things would be that way again, after she healed.

"Time was that all recruits were subjected to rigorous training and tests of faith," Virgil said, continuing through the shafts of damp light. Wooden doors with plain handles lining the left side of the corridor were closed and unmarked as though forgotten. "But as our number has dwindled we have had to become more accepting." Virgil stopped for a moment. "In fact, your father was instrumental in that change." He peeked at her from over his shoulder. The light behind caught the top of his head like a burst of smoke. "He was adamant that women be allowed to join." He looked down upon Riley, the shadow of his long nose hung over his lips. "He knew you'd be the one to carry on." He turned and started forward again.

The noise of training in the main chamber fell away. Virgil alone led her through the light and toward the darkness. "Today, only one of our original rituals remains. The most important and the most demanding."

"A math exam," Riley muttered to herself.

Virgil stopped once more. He angled his head to look at her through eyes she couldn't see. "This isn't a time for levity, Ms. McKnight. You are entering into a covenant from which there is no withdrawal. The blessing you receive today is not without its consequences. Even our strongest have experienced certain . . . troubles."

"You're doing a great job selling club membership."

Virgil chuckled once. "But, should you emerge unsullied, you will experience the world in ways very few in history ever have. You will be the light in the darkness. The guardian against the evil that brought ruin to our beautiful world."

"See things no one else can see," she said, "do things no one else can do."

There was an audible sigh as Virgil stopped again.

"Wind, fire, all that kind of thing," Riley said.

Shadow covered him as he turned to her.

"*Big Trouble in Little China*," she said. "You should see it."

Shadows grew longer as he dropped his head. "If you were anyone else, I would not display such patience." He stared down at her again. "If not for his legacy."

"I'm here," she said. "That should be enough."

"The corruption will not be subdued by your mere presence."

"You keep saying that. 'Corruption.' What is it?"

He straightened himself until he was little more than an outline to her.

"To the outside world it would be labeled a genetic mutation. They call it *lycanthropy*, from the Greek words for *wolf* and *human*. But, the few of us who know recognize the corruption for what it is. Divine judgment. The curse of God." Riley squinted to see through the light and shadow. "When did you last attend church?"

Riley pictured her father's funeral. "It's been a while."

She heard his feet squeak on the stone as he turned to continue on.

"Do you believe your father was a good man, Ms. McKnight?"

"Of course I do."

"Did you trust him?"

She didn't answer.

"Then do you not trust that anything which resulted in his death would be evil?"

"My father was not corrupt."

"That's right," Virgil said, spinning to her so quickly that Riley had to catch herself from falling. "But one doesn't need to be corrupt to be slain by the corruption."

She steadied herself on her crutches once more.

"Our order was founded on the principle that while this corruption would endure as long as humankind exists, it could be contained. Contained enough that the innocents, the lambs, could live without the fear of predators among them."

"And who decides who the predators are?"

He lifted his head into the light. The deep lines were tiny cracks in the glow. His eyes were reflecting pools. "A girl your own age. A boy and his entire family. Hunted, Ms. McKnight. Murdered. Just like one of our brothers. These are the acts of a predator. This is the corruption at work." The shadow of his chin fell all the way down his body, nearly extending to the floor. "The same corruption which claimed your father. The same corruption which killed your companion and left you broken."

She locked her jaw, staring up at him.

"Evil, Ms. McKnight, can never be forgiven."

She fell back into step as Virgil moved on. The end of the hall came into sight, another plain door set into another stone wall.

"Beyond this wall lies the means by which we contain the corruption. It is how we protect ourselves against evil. It is what separates us from beasts and lambs alike. It is God's last gift to the faithful, that we may serve his judgment on this world. That we may make it beautiful once more."

"I'm not here for dogma, remember?" Riley said, pausing a few feet back from where Virgil continued toward the door. "Nor your preaching, or faith. I lost that when the person I had faith in was taken from me."

Virgil turned again, behind the last light where shadow covered him.

"You promised to fix me. Promised that I'd be better than I ever imagined. Scientology promises the same thing without the sword fights," she scoffed. She leaned forward to place her crutches on the stone and swung her good leg out. "You asked if I trusted my dad. You're damn right I did. But just because you have his picture hanging in your clubhouse doesn't mean I trust you."

"Your father lied to you, Ms. McKnight. Lied to you your entire life. This place, this . . . city . . . was created as a sanctuary for wolves while we, pilgrims, are the shepherds watching over the sheep. Your father, our Father as well, was one such guardian." The shadowed figure stepped forward until the last patch of light cascaded over him. "As am I. I am a guardian of these people, of this town, and this world. And I am your guardian. I have known you your entire life, Riley. I knew you through your father. Knew you through his successor. And now, I know you through who you are. I watched over you in his absence. That's how I was able to find you that night, pull you from the wreckage that claimed that innocent boy. I made a vow that you, Riley McKnight, daughter and heir to the legacy of Clarence McKnight, would be my successor, the next to stand guard over this town, and hold the predators from the prey."

Virgil exhaled heavily. He shook his head. He shrugged, or at least that's how Riley saw him. For a moment, he seemed to have doubt.

"I understand your skepticism. I understand your lack of faith. I, too, have . . . questioned my place in this world. I, too, have been tested." He straightened, regaining confidence. "The man you had faith in had faith in me to usher you toward destiny. The man you trusted, trusted me."

Riley turned away. The gymnastics classes, the insistence that she do things for herself, the military jacket, even his favorite overused quote, everything she could remember of her father seemed to point at him pushing her toward . . . something. Perhaps it would have been clearer if he'd had more time.

"Riley," Virgil said. The light in his eyes peered directly at her. "I promise you, here and now, that if I ever betray your trust, you may strike me down."

Riley felt herself sink. "What about my mother?" she asked after a silence.

"Your mother was heartbroken. I was there when Father Innocent spoke to her about all Pius had done for us, for this town and its people. For the entire world. She was furious, but she understood. I haven't spoken to her since. Maybe she would approve of your being here, maybe she wouldn't, but you can't let her make this choice for you."

"Yet my father should?"

"No," Virgil said, his face going pale and blank. "You should. You *have*. You chose to come here over and over, even after I told you not to. You could have turned away anytime, yet you choose to follow me here. Now, if you choose to go no farther, that is your choice."

The light burst as he turned his back to her. He

disappeared as he stepped toward the door, turned the knob, and walked into the dark within.

Riley took a deep breath. She peered back down the long hall they'd just walked through, pools of light flickering on the floor. Her legs ached. The pads of each crutch dug into her armpits. She pictured the scars on her face. Her father had one as well. She remembered the line he would quote to her. He was right, she couldn't handle the truth. Not as a child. But now . . . now . . .

The room beyond the door smelled like the change jar Riley's mother kept on top of the refrigerator. The metal was so dense it crawled up her nose and tugged at the front of her head.

"Come," Virgil said.

The light outside barely permeated the dark inside. Riley squinted to make out the vague shapes she saw before her. There was a creak as the door closed behind her. Complete black flooded over her.

"Don't worry."

Virgil's words sent a wave of terror down her

spine. He was so close she could feel his breath. A wounded girl alone in a dark room with a strange old man. She reached back with one crutch until it found the door.

"Your eyes will adjust." He was now far away.

A churning sound filled in the silence. Nothing else emerged from the darkness.

"Here," he said. "Put out your hands."

"What?" The smell was strong from his direction.

"Everything will become clear soon."

She felt his rough hand grab hers, turn it palm-up, and place a flat-bottomed object into it.

"This is your sacrament," he said, grabbing her other hand from the handle of her crutch. He placed it where the object rounded outward.

She leaned closer to see. In her hands was a cup with a thick stem leading to a wide bowl. The inside was too dark to see, but it was thick with the scent of old coins.

"What the hell is this?"

"This is our true weapon." His voice came from a

few feet away. "This is our truth and our faith. This is how we stand guard against evil. How we restore our world. This is not only how you fix yourself, but a promise that you will never be broken again."

"None of that answers my question."

"It is a taste of the corruption, McKnight, that we may know how to fight it."

It was stupid. Riley knew it was stupid. Yet something—obligation, curiosity, naivety, or the fact that she too was stupid—kept her from throwing the cup on the ground, slamming the door open and running as best as she could back down the hall, up the stairs, to her car, and straight to the police. She probably wouldn't make it anyway. She'd be caught, perhaps even forced into drinking whatever it was, or worse. She had to accept that possibility.

"You've come this far," Virgil said, several more feet away. "If you can't have faith in our cause at least have faith in yourself."

She sniffed the cup once again. It was pennies and dust.

"After today, all your pain will be brief. Darkness will run from you. Fear will be a memory."

She shook her head at the scent.

"It smells worse than it tastes."

"Really?" she asked.

"No," Virgil replied. "It is awful, but it is worth it."

Riley sighed. It was too late now. "What the hell."

A stinging metal taste hit her tongue. The warm, thick liquid coated her mouth. It burned into the base of her teeth. She felt hot needles in the back of her throat and nose. Her eyes watered as she choked. She coughed some of it out.

"For the life of the flesh is in the blood," she barely heard Virgil say.

She squeezed her eyes shut and strained to tilt back the cup. She shook as she swallowed.

"And I have given it for you on the altar to make atonement for your souls . . . "

She gagged. She scratched her tongue against

her teeth, trying to remove the heat and metal that coated her mouth. She slowly reopened her eyes.

" . . . for it is the blood that makes atonement by the life."

Colors exploded before her. The stone walls bore more shades of brown and gray than the total of every color she had seen before. Every nook and knot of the wooden tables lining the walls were as clear to her as they would be if she were an inch away. She could see residue along the rims of the old barrels placed on top of the tables. She heard the churn at the back of the room, a large gear under a heavier table holding up a large tub, as though she were standing right next to it.

Virgil stood in the center of the room several feet away. His arms were folded patiently. Every line and crack on his face appeared to her clear and sharp, without blur or shadow, as though a light were placed directly in front of him. Not the damp lights outside or the harsh lights on the street, but a clear light which seemed to bathe everything before her in clarity. His high-collared shirt gleamed like a pearl. Cracks on the back of his hands were tiny slivers. Every thin strand of hair pulled back from his high forehead was clear, down to the roots and follicles they sprouted from.

"Holy crap," she said.

"Is it?" he replied. His shirt was dozens of shades of white.

She surveyed the walls again, feeling as though her brain was swimming in color.

"Do you see now?"

She nodded.

"Good."

Virgil stepped forward to within a few feet of her. He lowered to one knee. The slight lines between the hairs on his head were distinct channels, like a map of crisscrossing streams.

She felt the cup still in her hand. The residue was the same as along the barrels' rims. She hadn't even noticed that the metal sting lingered in her mouth. Her leg and arms no longer ached. She pushed down on the crutches that supported her. There was a weightlessness to her movement. She pressed her boot to the floor. There was no pain. She leaned slightly. There was a slight pinch and nothing more. Not completely healed . . . but getting there, quickly.

Virgil remained on one knee, his head lowered. He lifted his right hand into the air.

"Lord, we grant your servant the name of Sapphira, and welcome her as a sister of the Order of the Hidden Blade."

Riley could see just inside the cuff of his pearl-hued shirt. She focused on the color, the way it shined out. The material of the sleeve started to fade, leaving the outline of a dozen white hues in its place.

"May her justice be swift and true."

Large green-blue veins tracked up his forearm. Indent marks remained in his skin, likely from years of wearing the wrist blade beneath his sleeve.

"May she be worthy of the trials fate has laid before her."

Farther down the inside of his arm, between the long-healed scars, were other lines—letters—cut into the flesh. *Liam Bailey.*

"By the blood we are bound."